Gone and Back Again

by Jonathon Scott Fuqua

Soft Skull Press
Brooklyn, NY
2007

D1360580

Gone and Back Again

Copyright © 2007 by Jonathon Scott Fuqua

ISBN 13: 978-1-933368-77-1

Interior design by Kate Larson and Nora Nussbaum
Cover design by David Barnett
Cover photo by Michael Gerwe (mgerwe.com)

Soft Skull Press
55 Washington St
Brooklyn, NY 11201
www.softskull.com

Library of Congress Cataloging-in-Publication data avaiable from the Library
of Congress

For Gabriel, because your whole strange boyhood is ahead of you. See the humor, don't eat too much free food, and tell your father if he starts quoting General Macarthur's "credos to live by" one day and wearing tweed suits the next. I love you dearly.

Acknowledgements

First, I need to thank my family, always. They aren't pandering, simple, or always easy, but I love them more than words can say. I thank my parents, and my brother and sister, who have been as integral to my early survival and current success as any siblings could possibly be for a brother who was, sometimes, not normal. I thank my editor, Jody Corbett, who came across this crazy manuscript and fell in love with it. How can I express my gratitude? Lastly, I thank Richard Nash at Soft Skull Press for taking risks in an industry often averse to them.

Chapters

A Start to this Story

Prologue

From here in Naples, Florida, in our new house, in my new bedroom with its window screen that always has a bright colored lizard crawling across it, I have wondered when my problems started.

I remember getting insomnia even before we left Yorktown, Virginia two years ago. Back then, after my parents' divorce, I'd sometimes find myself awake and nervous long past midnight. I'd walk around the house scared to stir anyone but dying to hear another voice. I even picked up the telephone and listened to, "If you'd like to make a call . . ." I was glad to hear the question.

Still, I think I was mostly okay. I laughed with my brother Fulton and my sister Louise, and even though I was only eleven I had a crush on a girl named Mary Doyle down the street. I loved to watch her misformed teeth move when she talked to me. When I was around her, I acted as entertaining as a sitcom character. At the same time, my family-life situation was slowly turning into a small disaster.

During the country's bicentennial party, my mom and dad first separated. Exactly one year later they were divorced. A few weeks after that, my dad got engaged to annoying Kora, the lady he'd been caught cheating with. He told us that Kora completely understood him so much better than my mom ever had. But as soon as my mom started liking Henrico, my dad seemed to want her back.

It was screwed up. But I didn't care. I wanted my dad to remarry my mom so that Henrico, who was a total jerk to us kids, would leave. That's why, when my dad asked me to tell him bad things about the man, I figured it was because, after a year-and-a-half, he wanted to win my mom back. I thought he was planning to come home.

"Like what do you wanna know?" I asked.

"Like how dagum bad a person Henrico is, Little Buddy." My dad took a sip of his beer, adjusted his hunting hat, and steered us around an interstate off-ramp and onto Mercury Boulevard. He loved to drink and drive, especially when he was acting like a Southern grit, which was one of his favorite selves. See, my dad was a completely different person all the time. Sometimes he was nice and sometimes he was angry. Sometimes he was a redneck and sometimes he was like a person from London. He was always changing. It was strange.

I told him, "Well, I mean, the worst thing is that he hates us. He hates us like crazy. And he acts important."

That didn't seem to impress my dad.

"Also, he tried to throw away my skateboard and took my fishing knife for himself."

"He's a thief, Slim?"

"A huge one."

"You know'a anything else he took?"

"Yeah," I said, thinking. Nothing came to mind, so I decided to lie. "Ah . . . he swiped Fulton's stereo, and I saw him take something off a store shelf."

"Well, he must be an old fashioned con, eh, Buck?" Dad finished his Miller Light. "Ya mind telling me? Does it seem like he's spending his money, or do ya think he's spending yours?"

I told him, "I don't have any money."

He pulled into the Coliseum Mall parking lot and headed the car toward J.C. Penney's. "Yeah, ya do, Hoss. I give your momma loads of child support money every month. But I got myself a feeling Henrico's making off with it."

I gave it about a second's thought and said, "I bet he is. 'Cause he's just a cook, and Mom doesn't give us anything, ever, and Henrico's owns a fancy-type car and just bought a color television where he watches *Hawaii Five-O* on Sunday."

"God," my dad sneered, "he's a parasite."

"Yeah," I agreed.

Now, I'm not trying to make an excuse for my bad decisions, but anyone could tell that the information I gave my dad was mostly invented. Henrico was bad but in a different way than I made him out. My dad, being my dad, though, ignored my obvious lying and kept notes on everything I uttered. Then, when the time came, he used our private conversations and all my nasty comments in court, where a judge decided he could stop paying my mother alimony and shrink our child support to nearly nothing. That had been his plan. It wasn't to remarry my mom. It was to save some cash.

When my mom and Henrico got home after getting pummeled in court, you could see that they verged on hating me, which was scary.

"Your father used all of the bad things you told him about Henrico in court. Everything, a lot of it lies! So tell me, what were you thinking?" she asked. "What were you thinking!" she yelled, her face red and wrinkled with rage.

Ashamed, I said, "Nothing, Mom!"

"Well, you've pushed this family over a cliff. Do you recognize that?"

"I just talked to Dad. I—I didn't mean to do anything."

"You said I don't ever buy you things."

"Not . . . so much stuff. Do you think?"

"How about your food? How about this house? How about your doctor's bills and your school clothes?"

"Oh, yeah," I mumbled.

"You told personal information."

Henrico pointed at me. "You goddamn bastard!"

I turned to look at him. He'd changed our lives, and I hated him for that. "You're the bastard," I rasped, amazed at myself.

My mom grabbed my arm. "Just get out of here, Caley! Go to your dad's and don't come back 'til you can say you're sorry."

Surprised she was kicking me out, I did what she wanted and stumbled through the side door and across Yorktown to my dad's apartment. Sadly, he and Kora were celebrating his court victory and smashed out of their minds on booze, so he didn't want me there. "Go on back to your momma's," he directed, shutting the door in my face.

I walked back. Of course, I hadn't meant to make my mom mad or get her money taken away, so when I arrived at the front door I said, "Sorry," and then started burping uncontrollably for two weeks.

The burping sounds like a joke, but it was bad. I tried to stop but couldn't 'til, finally, my mom got worried. In the kitchen one night after she forgave me, she looked me in my eyes and shook her head. "Cay, do you think it's something you're eating?"

"No. I'm eating normal." *Burp!*

"Is there anything in your throat?" With soft fingertips, she felt at my windpipe. "How's your stomach?"

"They're both okay." *Burp!*

"We need to take you to the doctor's, sweetheart. Do you know that?"

"I figured, yeah." *Burp!* "I'm burping too much."

"You are."

A day later, we were sitting in Dr. Houseman's office. Dr. Houseman never gave out medicine for anything. He came out and directed my mother to stay in the waiting room as he took me into his office. Sitting, he looked at me.

"Yeah?" I asked. *Burp!*

He asked, "What's wrong?"

"Can't stop burping." *Burp!*

"You can't?"

"No, Dr. Houseman. I just keep doing it." *Burp!*

He leaned forward. "Very strange."

"Is it common?" *Burp!*

"It is very uncommon, Caley. But, I don't think you're sick."

"You don't?" *Burp!*

"No. Caley," he said, "I think you can quit right now."

"I can't," I told him. "It's like something's broken." *Burp!*

"Stop burping. Stop making yourself burp."

I stared at him like he was an idiot. "I've tried for like two weeks." *Burp!*

"Stop now," he said.

"But . . . ," I started to reply.

"*But* nothing. Everybody is tired of hearing burps."

"They are?"

"Yes."

"Okay," I mumbled, and stopped.

I didn't know I could, but I could. Now I see that burping was like turning down the first block on the strange road my brain decided to take. Even now, I wish I had gotten something regular like hives instead of unregular like burps. Maybe if I had, things would've been different. Or maybe it was all going to happen and I couldn't do anything about it.

In Yorktown, a few weeks after the burping disaster, my mom and Henrico surprised the world and got married in our living room. After kissing—a disgusting sight to see—they announced that we were moving just down the interstate and across the bay to Norfolk so that Henrico could open a fancy restaurant.

That night, halfway through the wedding dinner of tuna casserole, Fulton, who was fourteen then, put his fork down and told them, "You know what? I don't want to move."

I looked up, hoping that his calm statement might change my mom's and Henrico's mind. I had been born in Yorktown, and I had a crush on Mary Doyle down the street. I didn't want to go either, but I knew nobody would listen to me. I was only eleven.

Henrico said, "Tough."

"But, really, I don't want to."

"Tough crap, Sherlock.'"

Fulton picked his fork back up. "Thanks, Henrico."

"You being a smart aleck?" he asked threateningly, and that was the end of it.

When we finished eating, me, Fulton, and Louise cleared the table and met in the television room in the basement section of the house.

Like spies who might be killed if the wrong person heard us talking, we turned up the volume on the TV, shut the door at the top of the steps, and whispered about how much we hated the idea of moving to Norfolk.

Fulton said, "That's it. I'm not going. There's a hollow tree in the woods I found last year. It's where I keep my cigarettes, and it's got everything I need to live, so I might just escape from home and go there to stay since I hate Henrico and don't want to move. I'm not kidding."

Louise said, "Does it have a toilet?"

"I can go outside and use leaves."

"How about a door? Does it have a door?"

"I don't need a door."

I said, "What happens if it starts to snow and the wind blows the snow in?"

"I'll take some blankets," he told us as some kids on a television commercial started singing, "I'd Like to Buy the World a Coke," making me wish they would so that I could have one and get rid of my dry mouth, which was annoying.

I wondered, "What happens if a bear comes to the tree and wants the spot more than you?"

"The only bears left around here are practically tame, so I could scare it off by waving my hands."

Louise gasped, "Yorktown's got bears?"

"I think," I hissed to her, hushing her with a finger to my lips. "You know what I might do?" I told Fulton.

"What?"

"It doesn't sound as good as your tree, but I might go beg to Mom for us. I might beg to her for us to stay here and divorce Henrico since we all hate him but her. Do you remember, sometimes if we used to beg her, she'd do things?"

"Beg?" Fulton said like the word tasted bad. "Beg? That's pathetic. Begging makes people look weak, Cay. You wanna look weak?"

Louise whispered, "Yorktown's got bears. I can't believe it."

Fulton frowned at her. "Shut up, Louise, huh? Maybe there aren't any anymore. We don't know."

She asked, "How about mountain lions? Do we have mountain lions?"

I explained to her, "We mostly got deadly snakes, okay?"

"And rabies and mosquito-borne illnesses like diarrhea," Fulton added.

I watched a kid eat cereal on a television commercial before looking Fulton in the eyes. "Oh, yeah. When you're in your tree, what are you going to do about mosquitoes, Fulton?"

He shrugged.

"They'll suck you dry. Plus, in the summer, how will you keep a fan going so you don't sweat to death?"

Fulton frowned at me. "I totally forgot about sweating. I totally forgot how I hate sleeping sweaty."

Louise cupped her hands like the front part of a horn and said to Fulton, "Now you aren't going to live in the tree?"

"No. Probably not unless I can get a really long extension cord to run a fan."

"You'd still need somewhere to plug it in," I reminded him.

Louise sat in a beanbag chair. "Cay, now you gotta go beg Mom."

"Right now?"

"Yup," Fulton told me.

Wishing I didn't have to, I went upstairs to where she was doing her wedding night dishes all alone in the kitchen. That's where I asked her about divorce and that's where she got really pissed at me for not allowing her a few hours of peace.

The next day, when we carried the news about the marriage and the moving to my dad, he took it even worse than mom had taken me ruining her quiet, wedding dishwashing time. Driving toward Kora's house, he put his head against his steering wheel and floored the gas petal so that we flashed by other cars. "God. I—I don't have anything to live for. Nothing," he moaned.

"Yeah, you do, Dad," Fulton, who was sitting in the front seat, told him.

"Nope, I don't, son."

"You got your boat and Kora and her kids."

"Next to you guys, they don't mean anything." He raised his eyes and steered wildly past a dump truck.

Louise, who was eight, said, "We aren't gonna be far."

He glared in the rearview mirror at her. "How do you know?"

I answered, "Norfolk's just over the bridge. Also, Mom told us."

"Well, Caley," he replied, screeching around a corner, "we all recognize that your mom's a gigantic liar, don't we?"

Fulton snapped, "No, we don't."

"Well," my dad replied, "why did we get a divorce then?"

I wanted to say, "Because you and Kora were sneaking around passing love notes," but I didn't since he always acted like it wasn't about his cheating as much as Mom not being very nice and understanding.

Fulton said, "Dad, you're going super fast."

"So what? I got nothing to live for."

Because it sounded like he was going to drive us into a tree, which would be sort of selfish if you think about it, I sat back and tightened mine and Louise's seatbelts.

He didn't crash the car. Instead, he raced us back to our house and dumped us out front. Then he peeled out. As we walked to the front door and rang the bell, I wondered if he was going to kill himself. If he did, due to not murdering us along with him, his death would be a lot more tragic and sad.

Opening the door, my mom wasn't happy to see us. "Where's your dad?"

"He dropped us off."

"Already?"

"He didn't wanna take us to Kora's anymore," Louise explained.

I added, "He was too sad."

"Why?"

"'Cause we're moving."

"So he left you back here?"

"Yeah," Fulton told her.

"That selfish pig. We could've been out to dinner. He was just trying to be difficult. He isn't sad. I know he isn't sad."

I said, "He seemed a little sad, like he wasn't lying."

"Caley," she said, "stop defending him."

"I'm not."

"What were you doing then?"

"Just explaining."

"You don't ever think your father does anything wrong, do you?"

"I do."

"Just go upstairs," she said to me.

In my room, I remember thinking how my mom had once treated us so wonderful and didn't anymore. She'd changed after the divorce. It was like her goodness and affectionateness seemed to be hibernating or were gone.

After living in Yorktown our entire lives, we were leaving and there was nothing me, Fulton, or Louise could do. Our last night in the area, my dad, who hadn't killed himself, came and picked us up for our "going away dinner." Being that I was so down, I remember wanting it to be a special, really sad night. On television, if you watch, sadness always brings everyone's honest love to the surface of their skin. On television, sadness can seem sort of nice.

But, it wasn't nice. My dad took us to the Western Sizzlin' Steak House, and we ate our steaks and drank our Cokes almost silent 'til he started in on feeling sorry for himself, which made me want to spit steak bits all over him.

"You'll stop loving me. You'll forget I ever lived on this planet. You'll forget, and I'll be gone from your life and all alone." He poured out some A-1 Sauce on his plate.

Fulton told him, "No, we won't. We'll only be forty minutes away. If you go fast, it's less."

"Might as well be six hours."

"That's not true," Fulton said.

"Yeah, it is. Kids, the truth is that Henrico wants to be your dad now. Did you know that?"

Fulton snickered at that comment. "You're wrong about that."

Alongside my dad, I couldn't help chuckling, too. Luckily, he didn't see me.

He snarled at Fulton, "Son, sit up straight and don't eat with your grubby fingers."

Following our dinner, we had pudding and left for home. Before getting on the Yorktown Parkway, though, he stopped at a service station and asked me if I wanted to pump gas. Well, of course I did, even if he was being nice to me in order to get back at Fulton for laughing at his comment. Thrilled, I removed the gas cap and flicked the switch on the pump.

Halfway through, my dad said, "Your mom wouldn't let you do this, eh, Cay?"

"Mostly she doesn't get self-serve."

"Of course she doesn't. I've been paying her too much money, is why. You wait to see what she does now."

"Okay," I told him, not wanting to talk about that stuff.

With the gas tank full and the windows cleaned off, my dad took us home. Riding in the backseat, I was nearly goofy with joy. Smiling softly, I decided that the evening had been better than I thought at first.

In front of our house, he burst into strangled tears and gave me and Louise strong, blubbering hugs like never before. He didn't give Fulton a hug, though, or even look at him, not 'til Fulton noticed that the car's gas door was open and the cap was missing.

Looking sick, my dad said to me, "Did you put the cap in your pocket, Cay?"

I shook my head. "No, sir."

"Did you screw it back on when you were done?"

"I—I thought I did."

"Did you forget?"

"'Cause I never have pumped gas before, maybe."

"God, Almighty."

"Sorry."

"Caley, what were you thinking? Or were you thinking? Or maybe you planned it."

"I didn't."

"The hell you didn't. You can't leave well enough alone, huh?"

Fulton, who was angry at me, didn't say a word in my defense. But Louise went from crying sad to crying miserable.

"Caley, just go on and go. Get out of here!" my dad roared. "Backstabber," he called after me.

Hating myself, I got to the end of the sidewalk and rang the bell. One last time, I felt my pockets wishing for the gas cap. If it had been there, I would've attacked my dad and tried to shove it down his throat for the way he had twice ruined my night, a night I'd wanted to be meaningful. It was my fault about the cap, but I hated how he thought I was out to ruin things.

I really did hate that.

For some reason, every time we move, it rains or snows. Even when the North American moving van company was unloading our furniture here in Florida, bad weather got us. A tropical depression snuck in around the bottom of the state and flooded mall parking lots while causing the palm trees to twist and coconuts to drop and dent car hoods.

On the day we left Yorktown for Norfolk, rain beat down around us as we started along past Newport News and over the Hampton Roads Bridge Tunnel. We drove down strange roads and turned into an unfamiliar neighborhood. We stopped in front of a not-very-nice-looking house, and my mom got out from the car and ran to the gray front door. She opened it and her knees wobbled beneath her.

Through a misunderstanding, she had rented us a home filled with worn out furniture. It ended up that we had to stick ours in storage, which wasn't a very good way to start somewhere new.

The second bad-way-to-start was arriving in the fall. The neighborhood was completely empty. Nobody was around and all the houses had their shutters latched closed. When we asked a lady at the grocery store why everything was barren, she said it was a summer vacation community and not a normal neighborhood, which made sense being that it was only six blocks from the Chesapeake Bay.

My mother assured us, "You'll meet kids at school."

A week later, Henrico's restaurant, El Taste de Europa, opened and started flopping. It turned out that nobody in Norfolk ate fancy food. To make things worse, my mom left to help Henrico at the restaurant one morning and barely ever came home again. In order to keep Fulton, Louise, and me from starving, she hired three different old lady babysitters to take her place. But they weren't any good. Mostly, they shuffled around the house not wanting to make us dinner or do dishes.

November came and it started getting cold outside. That was the third bad-way-to-start. In both our Yorktown homes, we'd had regular heat from vents on the floors and walls, but in our summer vacation cottage house in Norfolk, there wasn't a furnace. Instead, there were flat space heaters bolted to the walls above our beds, and if you weren't alongside them it was so cold you could breathe steam. On freezing nights, the heaters glowed orange and when you slept they cooked you nicely until bad dreams caused you to roll around so that you ended up pressing a shoulder or elbow against them. Then they weren't so nice after all.

Maybe it was due to so many snags that I didn't adjust well. I knew I was lonely and missed my old friends a lot. I also suddenly developed a strange medical glitch where, for some reason, I became allergic to ice cream and milk. If I ate them, or cheese, I'd get explosive diarrhea, even at school. Due to that, and being new, I think, nobody at school seemed interested in meeting me. I understand. Who wants to be friends with a new kid who's a huge crapper? I didn't, even though the huge crapper back then was me.

Meanwhile, the new neighborhood was like a ghost town, which didn't matter to Fulton since he's different. He always did fine. Within a couple of weeks, he was having fun becoming a drunk. He started chugging beer and skipping school with a bunch of kids he had met in afternoon detention at his junior high school. Usually, after dinner, he ignored our old lady babysitters' orders and left with his friends, while me and Louise went upstairs and watched television in the cold family room.

Being in Norfolk wasn't pleasant, but when my dad came and got us for a weekend in Yorktown, it got worse. To be more like a family during our visits, he told us we weren't allowed to see our old friends and had to spend time getting to know Kora's boys, Hugh and Barney.

Also, after a few months, he started picking us up late. If he was supposed to arrive at 4:00 in the afternoon, he'd arrive around 8:00 in the evening or worse.

One Saturday morning, after he'd forgotten us altogether the night before, he called to say he was on his way. Getting off the phone, I looked at my mom, who was leaving for the restaurant. She told me I should ask him why he hadn't called last evening. I didn't want to, but since I barely saw her, I felt like I should follow her orders. So when he arrived that afternoon—six hours later than he had said that morning—I was nervous but determined to say something.

Like always, me, Fulton, and Louise drew straws. I won and got to sit in the front seat of his new car, where right off I started tinkering with the glove compartment latch. After a few minutes of driving, he said, "Young man, are you determined to break that damn thing?"

"Sorry."

He didn't reply.

"Dad?"

"Yes, son?" He was speaking in a snobbish style that I recognized as his person-from-London personality.

"Dad. . . ah . . . ," I said. "'Cause you didn't call last night, we didn't think you were coming. That's what we thought."

"Of course I was coming."

"Well, it didn't seem like it."

"If you'd prefer, young man, I can turn around and deposit you back at your home, where you can continue your weekend without me."

"No thanks."

In the backseat, Fulton sat forward. "Why not? Go on and take us home."

Louise gasped.

My dad said, "Is that what you want?"

"Sure."

"Fulton, does your mother teach you any manners at all?"

He didn't reply, so I said, "She does. A lot."

"Not enough, it seems."

Fulton scoffed.

My father frowned in the rearview at him and drove sort of recklessly. A few minutes wobbled by, and he sneered, "Do you know what? Your mother ought to be in jail. She really ought to be in jail."

I looked along the interstate wishing we were at Pizza Hut or Shakey's, some place public where he couldn't get too mad, even if eating cheese pizza would cause me to explode.

Fulton asked, "Why should Mom go to jail?"

"For spoiling you kids to death."

At that, Fulton burst out laughing, which was just about the greatest thing he could have done.

Dad demanded, "What, son?"

"Nothing."

"I want to know what is so funny."

Fulton said, "Don't worry about it."

"Tell me!"

"It's nothing. I promise," Fulton told him, trying to avoid our father's temper.

"Goddamn it, talk!" he screamed and hammered his new car dashboard with a fist, causing it to split above the radio.

In the shocking quiet that came after that, Fulton's braveness evaporated. He said, "It's just, you guys hate each other so much. That's all."

But my dad, who was staring at the crack, was off the subject. He touched the long break with a finger. "Look what you made me do," he whispered.

I hated how he was so unpredictable.

Nothing But a Blur

One Sunday in Norfolk, my mom woke up and didn't leave for El Taste de Europa right away. Henrico went out the door alone, and my mom, with her baggy eyes and face that seemed melted like wax near one of our bedroom heaters, stumbled into the kitchen. On account of not knowing where anything was, she started fishing around 'til she found a pan that had hard grease in the bottom from one of the old ladies not washing it.

"What're you doing?" I asked.

"Making pancakes, like in the old days."

"You aren't gonna go to the restaurant today?"

"I will later. Around dinnertime."

Louise woke up and came in dragging her filthy blanket that used to be clean. She hugged my mom's leg, and my mom touched one of her shoulders.

"Cay," my mom said wearily, "where's all the pancake mix?"

"Might be gone. Mrs. Lube makes them for dinner. She says that her upper and lower dentures require soft food."

She shrugged and fixed herself coffee.

"We aren't gonna have pancakes now?"

"How?" She took a deep breath. "I'll . . . ah . . . get us some eggs."

I nodded, thinking that the difference between pancakes and eggs was the difference between chocolate cake and a tomato. Whichever do you want, cake or a tomato? I was let down.

For breakfast, we sat at the dining table. I pulled my bare feet up in the chair and put my butt on top to keep them warm. My mom was so tired that she didn't talk, so I said, "I hate Sunday morning television. It's always religious shows. They're always saying, 'God, God, God, God, God.' You know? They always say it."

Louise said, "I wish Sunday shows were like Saturday cartoons."

My mom sipped her coffee and rasped, "So . . . ah . . . Cay, both Mrs.

Morto and Mrs. Ratchkey have been saying you don't ever talk. They say you only go into your room by yourself and never come out. Is that so?"

Still wishing the eggs were pancakes, I said, "Well, it's not exactly like that."

"What's it like, then?"

"I go into my room and play with figures. Later, I come out and watch television. Also, every morning I go to school."

"You think you need friends?"

What I hate about eggs is the yellow liquid that comes out from the yolk and gets everything dirty. With my fork, I was blocking it from spreading and concentrating on that. "Nobody lives around here."

"Couldn't you go home with someone from school?"

"It turns out that everybody at school hates new kids."

"That's not true."

"They all think I'm a Russian spy."

"You don't look Russian," she tried to joke.

"They all wanna drink milk, and I can't."

My mom said softly, "Cay, dear, I'm worried about you. Louise has made friends, and Fulton has made friends, but you haven't."

I nodded, and for a second wondered if she was finally going back to the way she was before the divorce, when she was aware if me, Fulton, or Louise felt sad or unhappy. But I only wondered for a second. I knew she wasn't. I could tell she was forcing herself to ask me questions. It wasn't what she wanted to do but something she had to do. "Maybe," she said, "you can do more with your brother? He's doing fine. I could ask if he'd let you follow him around?"

I stared at her. She had no idea that Fulton, who was still sleeping, skipped school and drank like my dad when he was driving. "I don't like Fulton anymore."

"Yes you do."

"Nah-uh."

"Stop."

I looked down at my soggy eggs.

"Listen, Cay, starting this week, I'm making it a policy that you two are going to work at the restaurant once a week, on separate days. We'll pay you a dollar an hour. It's because I want to see you. I miss you." She forced a grin. "Do you remember how much fun we use to have?"

"Yeah."

She pointed at me. "So, buster, you'll work once a week. Got it?"

"You want me to cook?"

"I want you to wash dishes."

The dishwashing area was about twenty feet from the stoves where Henrico worked, causing him to yell at me a lot. When he didn't, I wondered if we were becoming friendly. That feeling lasted 'til he banged his finger or over-cooked something and needed to holler. Since I couldn't quit the job, he hollered at me a lot. I didn't like that.

The good thing about working, though, was having money. I had so much I bought dozens of crappy toys at the local Woolworth's. I wasn't very choosy and got some really bad stuff. The worst was Stretch Armstrong, which, in case you didn't know, was a toy muscle man with rubbery arms and legs you stretched by yanking. After two weeks, I was so bored with him I cut his skin until stinky blue jelly came out.

What I really wanted was *Star Wars* action figures, but without my mom's help it was nearly impossible to get the good ones. When a nearby store had figures, they sold out of Luke Skywalker and Darth Vader and other popular ones so fast all I ever saw was Chewbacca, who is like a gorilla that can't speak, and C-3PO, a robot that acts girlish and prissy. I didn't want those.

Then halfway through the winter, before leaving for work, my mom showed me a newspaper advertisement. It said that the Military Circle K-mart was getting a shipment of *Star Wars* figures in on Wednesday.

"Can we go?" I begged.

"On Saturday."

"But the good ones'll be gone by then. That's the problem."

"It's the best I can do."

That evening, I asked our babysitter, Mrs. Morto, to drive me to Military Circle on Wednesday, but she said she couldn't because she had a leaky, unpredictable bladder.

Frustrated, I went out to a bus stop and grabbed a handful of schedules. After looking at them, I phoned my mom at work.

"Mom?"

"Cay?" she answered while somebody nearby yapped at her loudly.

"Tomorrow I wanna take a city bus to Military Circle Shopping Center. For the *Star Wars* figures. I've figured out the way. Is that okay?"

The person stopped talking in the background and she said, "What?"

I repeated myself as the person started yapping again.

When the person was done, she said, "You wanna take a bus?"

"Yeah."

"To where?"

"A shopping center."

"Fine," she told me. "Be good."

The next day, following school, I caught the number 67 bus to a transfer stop. There I got on the number 42 to a second transfer stop. After twenty minutes of waiting, I took the number 19 all of the way to Military Circle Shopping Center, where I ran to the Kmart.

Inside, I sprinted through the aisles to the toy section. Amidst a crowd, I found Luke Skywalker, Darth Vader, Obi-Wan Kenobi, Han Solo, and two stormtroopers. I even got Princess Leia's escape pod.

I paid and walked back to Military Highway. I was planning to retrace my bus ride back to school and then to my house. Unfortunately, I waited and waited 'til it got dark and a light rain turned to ice and my hands got wrinkled like I was in a tub. Finally, I went to a pay phone and called Mrs. Morto.

"Where are you?" she asked.

"At Military Circle. I think I'm stuck. Ah . . . what should I do?"

"Don't know. Your mom was worried. She phoned the police."

"She did?"

"Yes, you never came home from school."

"But I was getting *Star Wars* figures. I told her."

"Whatever. Where are you exactly?"

"Alongside the movie theaters."

"I'll let her know. Stay there." She hung up.

Worried, I squatted against the wall.

An hour later, Buddy, the gay waiter from El Taste de Europa, rumbled up in his pink Camaro with mag wheels. "Hey, Caley," he said in a lispy voice. "Hop in. I'm your chauffer tonight."

I got into his car but was too nervous to speak.

"Watcha got in the bag?" Buddy asked, turning onto Military Highway.

"*Star—Star Wars* figures."

"They're hard to get, I hear."

"Yeah."

He drove a few minutes.

I said, "Buddy?"

"Yeah, Caley?"

"I just got to know, do you really kiss men?"

He laughed. "I'm afraid so."

I got the chills. "How can you?"

"Because I like them. You don't have to understand."

"Okay." I waited a moment. "Is my mom mad at me?"

"She's relieved. She told me to tell you she'll call when you get home."

For dinner, I ate five cold fish sticks and a small mound of tater tots.

It was late, so Fulton had already gone off with his friends and Mrs. Morto was snoring in my mom and Henrico's bed. Tired, I went up to the family room and showed Louise my *Star Wars* figures. I put the bag down and got a big blanket around me while I waited for my mom to call. She didn't, and, eventually, shivering to death, I went to sleep.

The next morning, when I told her that Buddy wasn't completely gross for kissing men, she said, "What made you say that?"

"How he came to get me last night."

She stared into space. "He did?"

"At the shopping center."

She raised her eyebrows. "My mind must be slipping. The last four months are nothing but a blur." She shook her head.

"But you even called the police," I told her.

"Wow," she said.

A Downward-Going Kid

For me, life was like a train passing into a tunnel just before an avalanche falls and blocks the way out. Once we moved to Norfolk, I knew we had to go forward toward worse and worse, I knew that my past was lost and I might be, too. Still, a better kid would've been a better person. I became a huge let-down to me.

The winter was almost done, and I was nearly twelve. I was supposed to start junior high in the fall, except I wasn't sure I'd get out of sixth grade. I had quit doing homework and was failing tests in every subject. I never liked school, but my dislike was twenty times more since moving.

Also, I hated the restaurant for how it was flopping, and the sad feel it had whenever I was there.

Plus, I had no friends.

Plus again, if I ate ice cream or pizza I'd get stuck on the toilet.

As usual, I wasn't sleeping well.

Another problem was that I wanted my mom to be like a mom instead of just a woman we sometimes saw.

Last of all, I was annoyed at my dad for saying stuff like, "You know, I don't have you kids anymore, but . . . blahdy, blahdy, bladhy, Kora, Hugh, and Barney are great, and my life is wonderful . . . blahdy, blahdy, blah."

I hated that.

Still, by listing things I'm not trying to make an excuse for my terrible behavior. I did what I did, and it wasn't right, and I've got to live with that.

The day I started my days of badness, I rode the school bus next to Louise, like always. The entire way home, though, I was bothered by the kids in back who were laughing and bouncing on their seats. They reminded me of how I'd been happy feeling the same as them when I was younger, and how I wasn't anymore. Thinking about that scared me.

Outside, it wasn't sunny, but it wasn't overcast. At our stop, I got up and felt light-headed. Stepping down from off the bus, my heart beat fast and out of order.

Confused, I peered toward the bay. The gray clouds appeared stuck like spilled cement on a board. It was so dismal looking I nearly burst into tears alongside Louise. Then I pictured my heart seizing like an engine gear with a rock caught in it, and I worried I might fall down. If I did, I knew I'd start begging not to be me anymore.

I barely made it home, but, when I did, I decided to change my routine by saying to Fulton, "Can I . . . ah . . . can I come with you after supper? You mind?"

"Just don't be annoying."

"I won't be."

After eating, I followed him out the door and into the cold pitch blackness of our summer community. We walked along in silence so that halfway through the spooky, lifeless area I wanted to turn around and run back to watch *Different Strokes* with Louise.

Out of the neighborhood, we headed along Shore Drive, meeting up with three of Fulton's new friends. Together, the five of us went to the 7-11 and paid a man to buy us beer that we carried in bags to the beachfront. I remember looking into the sky and thinking, *If I have a beer, I will be evil.* So I didn't. Then, I thought, *Since I don't like anything, I'm already evil.* So I drank five.

The next night, I went with Fulton again.

After that, I don't know what changed inside me, but I followed Fulton whenever I could.

On nights when I worked at the restaurant, I wished I was drinking at the beach. On nights when Fulton worked, I wished I was at the beach, too. On the weekends when my dad drove us to Yorktown, my mouth watered, wanting to have some of his drinking-and-driving beers. Right away, my whole, pathetic self revolved around drunkenness. Nothing else mattered.

At school, my grades went so far down that the guidance counselor called me into his office. Chewing on a pen, he asked if I was feeling okay.

I said, "Do I really have to be a student 'til I'm sixteen?"

"That's right. So make the best of it."

I looked at his baldness and thought he couldn't teach me anything.

He said, "You know, Caley, life can be difficult."

"A little."

"Sometimes it gets so confusing that we need to take time out to understand it. Sometimes it's necessary that work and school take a backseat to that understanding. Tell me, are you assessing your life? Has school taken a backseat?"

Because it was a good excuse, I said, "Yeah, it's taken one."

"Okay, Caley. I'll talk to your teachers. But I want you to know, if ever you need me, I'm here."

"Yes, sir," I said, but letting me off the hook like that wasn't very smart.

That afternoon, after riding the bus home, I walked to the Shore Drive 7-11 and stole for the first time. I don't know why I did it, but I went straight in and slid Twinkies down my pants. It was as simple as that. Later that night, when I was drunk, I went back and took a Hershey's bar. Then I started lifting items from any store I could whenever I was hungry or wanted them.

Soon drinking and stealing became routine. Usually, I'd steal about five snacks after school then get drunk on beer in the evenings. The old lady babysitters must have known but didn't care. I was the kind of kid who, even if you wanted to, you didn't care about.

Also, soon, I couldn't stop. That was a weird thing to recognize, because sometimes I wanted a normal evening but had to get drunk. "No more," I'd whisper to myself, but there was always more.

Then, about two months into my crime spree, my mom, who was leaving for work, said, "I've got good news."

"What?" Fulton and Louise asked.

"We're buying a house."

Louise said, "In a real neighborhood?"

"Sure," Mom told her.

Fulton snarled, "Oh, crap. When?"

"We bought it yesterday. Unfortunately, Henrico had to sell his car, but we're moving in just a few weeks."

I nodded.

Fulton said, "For your information, I just started liking this house."

Mom took a deep breath. "We need a more stable environment."

He glared.

I said, "That's good," but, actually, nothing seemed good. I didn't feel one way or the other. I looked at Mom's nice face and it reminded me of an X-ray picture of how she used to look.

All day, I felt sad and uncomfortable. That afternoon, when I got off the bus, I wanted to feel better so I went down Shore Drive to a cheap clothing store where I stole a belt. Slipping it into my underwear, I wandered home and sat on my bed. Out in the television room, Louise watched a whole *Leave it to Beaver* before I unzipped my zipper and took the belt out.

Staring at it, I got the chills. I wondered how I ever thought a belt would make me happier. I mean, they go around your pants is all.

The buckle was brass and had "Yes" written on it in letters that curled like smoke. But the way it shined in my hands, I knew it was a bad luck charm, the type of belt a downward-going kid wears.

A wave of panic spread over me and I rushed outside, looked around, and buried the "Yes" belt in the dirt. I wasn't a church person, but I stalked around for a few minutes before I threw my head straight back and blinked into the sky that looked like an X-ray, too. A minute or so passed, and I said, "God, make me feel less terrible. Stop my crime spree, okay? Okay, sir?"

He didn't.

A few weeks later, we moved into our new house. I left the belt behind, buried in the yard.

Since Leaving Yorktown

If I'd have imagined what a skydiver who pulls his cord and the parachute comes out balled-up thinks, I bet it's, *I have just ruined everything.* That's what I was starting to think, too.

Whenever I was so drunk that the bed spun, I felt like a huge loser, meaning I felt that way a lot. Uncomfortable, I'd rise from the covers and stagger around my new room wishing I was the me before my parents got a divorce—the good, undrinking me.

Everywhere, but especially at the beach—where everything is supposed to be relaxing—I started feeling separate from myself and the world. By the water, I squinted out at the springtime waves that rolled in soft against the shore and watched kids pat together castles and moats with buckets and shovels, and it made me feel like nobody could save me, that I was doomed.

My shame became so large it seemed like a person sitting beside me at the table, a person who could develop their own special medical glitches separate from mine.

At least my mom picked a good house for us to try to get stable in.

It had regular heaters and was located in a real neighborhood where a kid from my school lived down the street. His name was Curtis, and he had a face that curved inward like a teaspoon. It didn't matter because he was friendly and had a little brother named Thor after the Viking god who carries a hammer. A week after we moved in, I asked Curtis why Thor was named that. He didn't know. I also asked, "Do you ever drink?"

"Like soda?"

"Like beer."

He shook his head. "Dad would kill me."

I was glad for him.

After school, I started throwing the football with Curtis. It was fun. When we finished, I'd go back to the new house and sit on the screen porch feeling lonely and waiting to get drunk. There was a certain good smell out there, like the old leaves in Yorktown. It made me want to be different than I was. But I knew I was already a permanent drunk forever.

During the last week of school, a teacher assigned us to write an essay about our future. That afternoon, even though I wasn't going to do the assignment, I went out onto the porch and tried to picture my upcoming life and couldn't. I changed chairs and tried some more and failed. Nothing came into my head but blankness. I thought, *Oh, my god, I have ruined everything by drinking beer and eating stolen snacks.*

It was so terrifying I wanted my mom to stick me in a juvenile delinquent home for boys who do stupid things. I wanted her to save my life.

❖

At the restaurant that evening, I could've asked Mom for help, but I was chicken. I also decided I liked beer too much.

Me and my mom sat alongside the waiters at a table in the empty dining room, and Henrico, who always had a snarling, lion-look on his face, stalked in and out from the kitchen grumbling to himself. Staring after him, Mom said, "I don't know how much longer we can hang on to the restaurant. We have no business."

Aching to go get drunk, I said, "Can I go then, so you don't have to pay me?"

"It still might get busy. You never know."

I looked at Buddy.

Buddy said, "Least you don't work for tips?"

"I guess."

He pointed a pinky at me. "You want me to show you something that's entertaining?"

"Okay."

He straightened and brushed the hair off his forehead. "Did you know that I'm wearing a toupee?"

I sat up. "You are?" I studied his hairstyle. "No way."

"I've only got a little real hair left."

"Can't tell."

"It's a good toupee is why. When I remove it, the real me is a rather gruesome sight. You wanna see?"

I nodded.

My mom said, "I'd like to get a look too, Buddy."

Standing, he grinned. "I only show kids." Waving me around the corner of the dining room, he slipped off his hair to reveal the most disgusting head-top I've ever seen. The skin was red and sweaty and covered with strands of gray that looked like run-over worms. I laughed hysterically.

"Strange, huh?"

"It's . . . so . . . gross!"

He giggled kind of lady-like. "That's why I hide it."

I went out and told Mom how Buddy looked without his hairstyle. "I swear, he's like a monster."

Buddy came around and said, "And you wonder why the toupee business is booming?"

"Not anymore," she said.

It was my best evening since leaving Yorktown, and I didn't even get drunk. Still, it didn't mean that things were getting better. It was just one good night that I liked to remember.

I hate to say it because it's embarrassing to say, but I love my mom and dad.

I love my mom for being my mom and not so painful to care about, and I love my dad for other reasons, even though loving him can hurt like a baseball batted into my chest.

The problem with my dad is his unpredictability. Like I said, all the time he acts like different and unpredictable people who do unpredictable things. In fact, the summer we lived in Norfolk, my dad's new erratic thing was that he decided to stop coming to pick us up altogether. He, instead, instructed us to take the Greyhound bus from downtown to a small stop on J. Clyde Morris Boulevard, near Yorktown.

One thing I can say for sure is that it's hard to stay glad to see anyone when you're traveling on a Greyhound bus, even if you love them—and especially if you don't know why you do.

Normally, if there wasn't a traffic backup, going from Norfolk to Yorktown in a car took forty minutes. On the Greyhound, the trip took three hours. And they weren't nice hours. They were three hours of resting your head on dirty seatbacks that showed all the soaked-in grease and grit from other people's heads. It made you want to barf, especially if you were hungover from booze.

When we arrived at the J. Clyde Morris Boulevard station, no matter who my dad was acting like, we annoyed him. He'd shake his head and if he was in his cowboy self, say something like, "You kids're looking a mighty bit shabby these days. It's a mystifying sight since I pay loads'a child support to your momma," which was a bit of an exaggeration. Then he'd add something like, "You wanna know what? With how you kids are, I'm wondering if we ain't actually related. That's what I'm wondering."

To shut him up, we always said something like, "I think we are, Dad."

After that, we'd climb into whatever new car he owned and rumble along to Kora's place. Once there, we'd spend a day and a night with Hugh and Barney. Me, Fulton, and Louise hated that. Hugh wasn't so bad, but Barney was a total idiot who liked bothering people 'til they wanted to tie him to a train track.

Kora called him Barney Boy.

Following dinner in the evenings, my dad always searched around the table and complimented Kora's cooking and Hugh and Barney's manners. It was annoying, since by complimenting their manners he was disapproving of ours. You could tell.

We visited my father about once a month, and on our second visit that summer, me and Barney were done even trying to be friendly to each other. That's why, I guess, he started teasing me about my clothes that were growing shabbier and more stained because the old ladies weren't good at washing. He also joked that my face was getting zitty and that Mom and Henrico were stupid for trying to own a restaurant. My dad and Kora were upstairs and the five of us kids were downstairs watching television when I shoved Barney Boy's chair so that he almost fell over backward.

He got up and squared off with me in a fistfight.

Hugh, who was mostly nice, said, "Stop it, guys!"

Fulton told me, "Knock him out, Cay!"

Louise stayed silent, her eyes like saucers.

Furious, me and Barney circled and slugged at each other, mostly missing. Barney, as big a jerk as he was, could kick my butt, but I didn't care. I hated him.

I snarled, "You still think they're idiots?"

"Yeah," he answered, and swung at me.

I kicked back at him.

Hugh tried to separate us, but we got away.

"Scuz," Barney said to me. "You're so slow I bet you won't get out of sixth grade. I bet . . ."

"Least I don't have a mom who steals dads, who's a big cheat!"

Barney pivoted forward and hit me right in an eye. The shot nearly sent me straight to the carpet. "Talk some more about my mom," he said. "Talk some more, when your dad's the cheat."

I didn't. My eye hurt too much. But I couldn't quit. I wanted to hit him once. Just once.

Dizzy, I maneuvered and maneuvered around him 'til I was nearly in a frenzy. Barney, maybe nervous about how I was acting, backed up against the television console. That's when, figuring he had nowhere to go, I closed both eyes, rushed forward, and sort of looped a pinwheel punch at him. The blow knocked him into the television and split open the spot on his forehead below his straight-across, mental-hospital haircut. Surprised, he stumbled over to a sliding glass door and sat holding his face and howling.

Of course, my dad and Kora were downstairs in an instant.

Barney looked at them and played like I'd nearly killed him. He leaned back and threw out his arms like Jesus coming off the cross. It was ridiculous. But at least I'd won the fight. If my dad was acting like a redneck or an army officer, he would like that. I glanced at him, hoping.

I never had that kind of luck.

Kora helped Barney upstairs, and my dad stayed down in the television room with me, Fulton, Louise, and Hugh. Slowly he turned and grabbed me by my collar. Pulling me close, he stuck his face against my temple like he'd become Dirty Harry, from the Clint Eastwood *Dirty Harry* movies. "You think you're something, Caley? You think you're cool?"

Shocked, I answered, "No, sir."

"You think you're strong?"

"No, sir, it's just he always . . . "

"How about if you shut up when I'm talking to you?"

"Yes, sir."

"You're so tough you want to go a round or two with me? Do you?"

I shook my head. "No, sir."

"Good, because I'd kill you. I'd make you wish you weren't ever born. So, do that again, huh? Fight again, Caley, and I'll beat you 'til you're a bloody spot. Get it?"

"Yes, sir."

He shoved me to the floor, picked up a shoe and threw it after me. "Don't ever!" he yelled.

I looked at him for a minute before rolling over to my stomach and crying like a kid. It was so embarrassing I wished I was drunker than hell so I didn't care I was bawling. But I wasn't drunk, so I cared, and it was terrible, especially with my dad and Hugh watching.

The next day, coming upstairs, I heard Kora declare, "They're troublemakers, Eugene. Pure trouble, and I'm tired of them. I'm tired of them disrupting our household."

"Me, too," he huffed.

"Well, how about adding this to your picture. I have not once burned bread, but I did today. How do you think it happened?"

"How?"

"One of your kids turned up the oven temperature."

He paused before saying, "Which one?"

"All of them or one, who cares?"

"I'll say something. Don't worry."

It wasn't true. Who turns up an oven to be mean? However, that afternoon, on the car ride back to the bus station, my dad turned off the classical music station, took a sip from a silver flask, and asked why we took pleasure in upsetting Kora and Barney.

Because he'd threatened to turn me into a bloody spot, I was still too mad to talk.

Fulton answered, "We don't."

"Please, son, don't proffer me such a fallacious retort."

"What?"

"Was it you who turned up the oven? Did you want to burn Kora's labors?"

"What?" Fulton asked again, confused.

My dad pointed at Fulton's image in the rearview mirror. "Don't be flippant with me. Don't engage me like a peer."

Fulton barked, "Engage! What do you mean?"

He scoffed and drove along silently, smoking a pipe like Sherlock Holmes. Without saying goodbye, he dropped us at the front doors and roared away.

Arriving in Norfolk, Buddy the gay waiter picked us up and carried us to our home.

Going inside, my head pounded and felt packed full of wild flapping birds. They smashed around in my skull as if they were dizzy and confused, and, from my hair to my toes, I was so miserable.

That night, sitting in a dark ditch, me and Fulton and two of his friends got crushed on beer.

After about ten cans, I said, "Guess what? Last week Curtis got a brand new moped, but his dad won't let me ride it. I have to watch him go. That's all I'm allowed."

Fulton declared, "Curtis oughta say, 'Dad, let Caley ride!'"

"Yeah," his friends agreed.

"His dad won't even let me in their house."

A kid named Arlen said, "I got a friend with an old man like that. He's annoying as crap."

"It's like I'm a criminal," I told them. Angry, I guzzled another Miller. When the beer was gone, we walked back to our house and sat in the driveway. Bored, Fulton lit a cigarette and said, "Did you hear, Cay? Mom says we might move again."

I stared at him. "Really?"

"Yup."

"We just got here!"

"I know. It's a pisser. We should've stayed where we were."

Agitated, I got up and wandered in tight circles. I don't know why. Then I stumbled over to our neighbor's side yard, where in the dark I started breaking the limbs off of the bottom of their Christmassy-looking pine tree. Fulton and his friends came over to help, and the four of us snapped branches 'til one of the neighbor's bedroom lights clicked on.

Scared I'd get caught, I ran 'til I was across from Curtis's house, where I stopped.

The garage was open and a light was on inside. I could see his new moped shining behind a taken-down basketball net. I stumbled up their drive and went into the garage. I gawked at the moped wishing it were mine. I got on it. I squeezed a brake and imagined riding. Just to see, I started the engine. Due to the engine being on and rumbling, I roared out of the driveway.

Flying along, I thought, *Dad wouldn't steal a moped. He never did things like this. He was perfect. No wonder he likes Hugh and Barney more.*

I looked over my shoulder as houses fell away behind. I laughed and roared around corners and down by the water and along a small road in our neighborhood that went past a creek. Rounding a curve at full speed, I hollered like a cowboy and the back wheel slipped on some rocks, throwing me to the ground so that I smashed an elbow and spun around in a circle.

Curtis's moped hit a curb, causing the engine to quit.

I got up, and my hurt arm hung limp. I lifted the moped and saw it was a little scratched with a small dent on the gas tank part. But it started. I was about to get on and carefully drive it back to Curtis's when Curtis's dad arrived in his pickup.

Mr. Hill threw his door open and leaped out so that his construction boots thudded on the road.

Glancing in the truck's passenger compartment, I spotted Curtis's spoon-face in the passenger's seat. He looked sick, so I said, "Curtis, are you sick?"

Mr. Hill got to me and snatched the moped. "You'll get a bill for the damage," he said, trembling with rage. "And, you come round my house again, I'll kick you 'til your nose bleeds. You got that?"

I nodded. "Sorry, sir," I mumbled, but I knew it wasn't enough.

"Don't show your face," Mr. Hill warned, and took the moped, lifting it into the back of the truck.

Curtis and his dad drove off, and I stood alone with my elbow that didn't work. Twice in two days, a grownup had threatened to beat me 'til I bled. Sad for that and everything, I looked at the stars that seemed like chopped bone parts on X-ray film, and I nearly wanted to die.

Weakness in People

When I was little I went on a boat trip with my father and Kora's ex-husband Stan. It was before Kora and Stan were divorced, but that's not why I'm telling the story. I'm telling it because after I crashed the moped, it was one of my first thoughts.

Stan, in case you want to know, was tall with a body like an egg over two legs. Because of his eggfulness, his shirts stayed tight to him like they were painted on, even the wrinkles.

I can't remember why we took that trip. Maybe it was for fishing or maybe it was for going away, but we were heading to a hotel on the Eastern Shore of Virginia. Up until the morning we left, Fulton was supposed to come with us. At breakfast, though, my mom saw a bad weather report and begged us not to go.

She couldn't convince my dad or me, but Fulton saw it her way and stayed.

The trip started out nice enough. I had about five A&W root beers, handfuls of nacho cheese Doritos, and two cans of bean dip. The waves weren't so big that you couldn't walk around on deck, so, for my dad, I went back and forth to the cooler to get him his beer and uncrack his beer-tops a few times an hour. Uncracking beer-tops was something I loved doing for him, especially when he was being his excited ship captain self.

By early afternoon, the day had turned ugly. The sky above reminded me of dirty water going down a drain. It kind of circled. Waves around us swelled huge. Their peaks broke into whitecaps.

For hours, we smashed our way toward the Eastern Shore. In all the rolling and slamming, Stan turned bright white, like a seashell, and started puking Doritos and beer over the side of the boat. I was sorry for him.

A little while later, it got so rough that Dad's boat started flying to pieces. Waves crashed down and eventually all four seats in the cockpit ripped free, their big metal bolts twirling like used shotgun shells. A wave hit sideways, and one of the seats was washed overboard and sank.

Stan yelled, "Eugene, are—are we going to make it?"

"This is nothing," my dad told him.

But it seemed like something. As many times as I'd been in storms, the seats had never gotten torn off and sunk behind us.

The day got older, and the bay got worse, making it so that at the top of each wave, the back of the boat came out of the water and the propeller buzzed before going back under. Down in the cabin, flashlights and fishing rods and both of my dad's little rifles were crashing about like pick-up sticks. I worried that the rifles were loaded, too, and that a bullet might shoot through the hull and send the boat to the bottom.

Hours into our trip, Stan kind of gave up. He wiped back his black hair and said, "Kora makes the best cupcakes. If you ever tried them, you'd say they were the best. I might miss those if we don't make it."

"Shut up, Stan!" my dad yelled at him.

I started shivering, and the bottom of the boat cracked loudly, causing the beer cooler to throw ice and Miller Light cans all over.

I was terrified, but I kept myself quiet. I tried drinking a Coke but chipped a tooth on the bottle. Putting the tooth fragment in my pocket, I closed my eyes and thought of my mom. I wished she could save me like when I played sick at school and she came and carried me home. I knew we were going to sink.

The front windows shattered, and Stan swept away the glass and moaned, "Kora didn't want me to go. She wouldn't allow the boys to come."

"She didn't want me to go, either," my dad told him as we nearly rolled over but straightened at the last second. I guess, because of almost flipping, I didn't remember his comment about Kora 'til they were engaged.

Time passed, and late that night, long after the cooler disappeared overboard and the boat's canvas canopy tore along the middle, we puttered down a dark creek and into port on the Eastern Shore.

"How was that, Cay?" my dad asked as he tied us to the dock.

"I chipped a tooth on my Coke bottle."

He looked into my mouth. "We'll get it fixed."

I waited a second and asked, "Did we almost die?"

"Hell, no, son. I was in control."

In our hotel room, Stan and my dad guzzled more beer and told stories about our trip. They talked about almost flipping like it had been a football play in slow motion. Excited, they turned on the television and told me to go to sleep, which I tried to do but couldn't without my blanket. Back then, I admit, I had a babyish blanket that I'd meant to pack but forgot.

An hour went by, and I sat up and said, "Dad, I—I forgot my blanket."

He frowned at me. "You want your blanket?"

"Yeah, but I forgot it."

He glanced at Stan. "He forgot his wittle blankey, Stan."

Stan cackled. "Ain't you old for a blanket?"

"Yeah," I said, embarrassed, but that didn't make me want it less.

He scratched his neck. "Jesus, how 'bout if you don't whine for once, Caley? Why don't you go to sleep and don't bother me?"

I nodded and put my head down. After not saying I was scared earlier, my dad was mad at me for wanting my blanket. That's how he always was. One slip and he didn't forget. A month later, he still talked about it. Sometimes he even made about fifty jokes in a row about my blanket.

Anyway, on the night I destroyed our neighbors' tree and crashed Curtis's moped, I thought and thought about that trip because, due to it, I knew my dad would never forgive me for the crimes I'd committed. Not including his own, he hates weakness in people. And I'd been weak with envy for Curtis's moped and weak with wanting to be drunk for beer.

Bruised and scraped so that parts of my elbow oozed clear liquid, I walked home from the crash and swore to myself I was done being a delinquent. And I was.

In the kitchen the next morning, Mom felt the area around my black eye—where Barney had punched me—and while she did, I confessed I'd gotten drunk the night before. I ended by saying, "You oughta punish me bad. I want you to."

But I could see she didn't feel like thinking about it. It wasn't a big issue for her. "You ever going to do it again?"

"No. Never," I swore, realizing that by the way I'd explained it she thought it was my first time.

"Okay, Caley. I understand."

"Go ahead and punish me? Please, Mom?"

She sighed. "Sweetie. I'm too tired. Besides, you're punishing yourself already." She cringed when she noticed my hugely swollen elbow, which later turned out to have a cracked bone. "Did this happen in your fight?"

"It was while I was drunk."

She nodded. "You need to put ice on it."

I followed her instructions but wished she hadn't let me off. Her anger would've helped make me feel better. Instead, I had to remind and remind myself that he wouldn't forgive me. If my dad learned what I'd done, he'd divorce me just like her. If he learned, I'd end up with only one parent, as if he had died from something that made his body vanish, like a fire or airplane crash.

After that, I undid my drinking personality.

I also quit stealing. And since I wasn't a thief anymore, I didn't like to be watched when I was in a store. When cashiers were suspicious of me, I always felt like I was guilty and wanted to take off my pants and show them my empty underwear and not-full pockets. I wanted to say, "I'm not a crook."

Even today, my conscience reminds and reminds me that I nearly ruined my future, that I killed a billion brain cells, and that I've been evil like someone possessed. Norfolk was a bad time.

In the evenings, except for when I worked at the restaurant, I stopped going out and watched television shows with Louise and the old lady babysitters. I watched the night that Elvis died and the news broke, causing Mrs. Morto to yelp like her weak bladder had gone off.

During the day, I played with my *Star Wars* figures and drew pictures of Batman swinging from his Bat-a-rang and Captain America avoiding bullets. I was trying to make up for being so horrible. I even wrote Curtis an apology note and sent him $24.00 for his moped. He didn't write back, but I understood he thought I was a prick. In our house, I was like a bear in a cage going back and forth, except I was more of a ferret.

By the end of the summer, I'd been sober for a month and was feeling better until the morning of my first day at junior high, when my mom told us, "Guys, we have to sell the restaurant."

Louise, who was ready to leave for elementary school, peered at the floor. "Mom, we aren't moving again, are we?"

"Yes, Loo Loo, I think we're going to have to. I'm sorry."

Fulton straightened up. "We're moving?"

"Yes."

"Again?"

"That's right."

"Well, fine," he said evenly, "I'm not going. I'm staying here! I'm getting adopted by some other family!"

"Hush," my mom said. "Hush, Fulton."

"Don't tell me to hush!" he squawked.

I didn't say anything. I was numb and wondered if another place might be better than Norfolk, where I had been so bad. My brain was scrambled from sadness, guilt, and having been drunk a lot.

Iffins That Was Henrico

Standing in the Greyhound bus station on J. Clyde Morris Boulevard, less than a year after we'd moved to Norfolk, me, Fulton, and Louise told my dad about having to move again.

He dropped his keys to the floor.

I told him, "The restaurant flopped."

He closed his eyes. "Who woulda figured?"

"I did. You could tell it was happening."

"Even I could tell," Louise said.

Fulton stayed quiet.

In a thick Southern accent, he told us, "I was being sarcastical, don't'cha knowed? From the start, I knowed that place was gonna go belly up. I knowed it."

"Nobody in Norfolk likes fancy food."

My dad frowned at me. "Everyone knowed that. Do ya actually believe your momma didn't?"

"Yeah."

"Well she did. She knowed. Anyway, it don't matter. Woulda happened no matter what."

Fulton said, "Huh?"

"Allow me ta let ya in on a little secret. You're not moving 'cause of the restaurant. You were gonna move even if it was a grand success."

I said, "I don't think we'd be going if El Taste de Europa had done okay."

"I'm telling ya here and now, son, you woulda moved."

"Why?"

"'Cause of me. That's it. That's all. I'm signing off." He rubbed his nose and closed his eyes as if he was feeling a deep, deep achy pain.

"It's not about you."

"Caley, don't ya know it's always 'bout me. For years, your momma's been trying to destroy me."

"Dad," Fulton spoke up, "it's got nothing to do with you."

"That's what ya think, Fulton. She's in your head and got ya b'lieving anything."

"We don't have any money," I said. "That's all."

"Oh, ya got money. I pay child support ever' month."

"Not so much, though."

He became furious. "Your momma tell ya that, Cay? Christ, she's unbelievable."

What I'd meant was that he didn't send enough child support to keep the restaurant going, but I didn't try to explain.

"This is a bushwhacking, clear as day," he informed us. "But I won't let her win. I done killed folk for this type'a deceit."

I looked at Louise and Fulton. We knew he'd never killed anyone and hoped he wasn't planning to kill Mom.

Rocketing back to Kora's, my dad checked and rechecked his mirrors like we were being followed. When we arrived, he stopped at the top of the driveway, got out and watched the road for a minute, like FBI agents were prowling behind us.

They weren't.

That night in the television room, butt hole Barney said to me, "Personally, I'm glad you're leaving. I'm glad you won't visit anymore."

"Me, too," I told him.

"I hope I don't ever see you again. And, please, don't send letters. Did you know you misspelled like five words on my birthday card. Five words! There were only twenty all together and you missed almost half." He glanced away to watch Cindy, the trip coordinator or something on *The Love Boat*, which was an awful television show. Before talking again, he waited for a commercial. "You're slow at learning, aren't you?" he said to me while a guy in a chicken suit sold cars. "You can't spell and you can't write. You know what LD stands for?"

"What?"·

"Learning disabled. It's a term for retards, and everyone who's not LD knows what LD stands for. Meaning, I guess, you're LD if you don't know."

"Shut up, Barney."

He shoved me. "I don't have to. This is my house and you're visiting. I get to say what I want."

Across the television room, Fulton, who was reading a science fiction book, glanced up. "Barney," he said, "liking *The Love Boat* is evidence that you're brilliant, is that what you think? Well guess what? It's designed and written for morons, except nobody tells the morons who watch it because they don't want to hurt their feelings."

"What?"

"This show is for total nitwits."

"It's *The Love Boat*, Fulton. It's good."

Fulton laughed. "That's what I'm saying. It's 'good' for people like you."

I smiled. One thing about Fulton is you really shouldn't mess with him.

When we got up the next morning, my father was religious and forgiving. Over breakfast, he told us in a soft, intelligent voice that he excused Mom and Henrico for their "inexcusable" behavior. Later, he took us to a local church, where we went into the graveyard and read headstones. He said that our great-great-great-grandfather had been a Civil War hero. "He dealt with loss daily, kids. He dealt with pain by looking to God for his strength and purpose. That's how this family will stay together. We will meet under the eyes of God. We'll find our way in his light."

On Sunday, we skipped church service and went shooting. Walking along the high cliffs that tumble down to the York River, my dad suddenly sprayed a log with buckshot. "What iffins that was Henrico?" he asked, smiling and back to being a redneck.

We didn't answer.

"He'd be dead. Dead and buried." Turning, he opened the breach on his shotgun and rested the barrel over an arm. "You guys recollect when you was little and somebody broked into our garage and stoled our rakes?"

Fulton told him, "I remember."

"Yeah, well, you remember how I bought me a carloada rakes and lined 'em up like breadcrumbs back ta the garage? Then, ever' night for a week, I hid myself inside. You remember that?"

"No."

"Well, that's what I did. I sat on a chair holding this here gun." He patted his shotgun, which he slid two more shells into. "Was hoping. Was really hoping and hoping that whoever done stoled our rakes would come back for the new ones. I woulda shot 'em dead in a second, even if it was a chick. You can't go stealing from me. You can't take from me and not spect me to get no revenge."

We nodded.

After blasting some rotten logs and old beer cans, he drank-and-drove us for hamburgers at the marina where he docked his boat, then he carried us to the bus station.

Three hours later, we arrived back in Norfolk, where we went outside to wait for Buddy to arrive. Tired, I leaned against the wall, and after a few minutes a mutt that was part beagle and covered with cowish spots on its body that were black and brown overtop a white background walked up and sat in front of me. I leaned down and put my finger out and she licked it. "Hey Louise, look," I called, and Louise came over and patted the mutt.

"Can we call her Punchy?" she asked.

"Yeah, that's cool."

Fulton turned. "If you check, Punchy's probably got mange."

I shrugged. "Me and Louise are gonna take her home. Mom and Henrico probably won't even notice."

"Well, if they do, Henrico'll stick her in a sack and throw her into the bay. And you know what, drowning's worse than starving to death."

"Shut up, Fulton!"

"It's true. That's all."

Actually, since then I've found out he's a little bit right.

I've sort-of-starved and I've sort-of-drowned, and I liked the sort-of-starving a whole lot more than the sort-of-drowning. At least when you're starving you can have diet soda and a pickle. When you're drowning, you're just going under.

A Place I'd Rather Be

A few days after El Taste de Europa officially shut its big doors, Mom told us that Henrico had five jobs offers from all over the country and even one in Europe.

"Where are they exactly?" Fulton asked, still angry about the situation.

"Well," Mom answered, "let's see, Belgium, Los Angeles, Chicago, New York City, Youngstown, Ohio, and Lake of the Ozarks, Missouri."

I blurted, "Belgium and California are too far from Dad." I was thinking about how heartbroken he would be. Since that first weekend when we told him about the restaurant closing, he'd gotten less angry and a lot sadder. The last time we'd been with him he could hardly even move to do anything except sip beer or, when he was being a redneck, eat a barbecue sandwich.

My mom said, "Okay, what about New York City or Chicago?"

A few moments passed, and Louise asked, "Aren't they so gigantic?"

She shrugged. "That's what Henrico and I thought. So, that leaves The Lake of the Ozarks, Missouri or Youngstown, Ohio. To put it bluntly, Missouri would be isolated but pretty, while Youngstown is an economically depressed city and very industrial."

Henrico took out a brochure and stammered through an advertisement for a place called The Lodge by the Lake. "'Situated on the rocky . . . ah . . . shores of Lake of the Ozarks, The Lodge by the Lake is a four star hotel known for its summer recreation. Surrounded by . . . world famous golf courses and nu-mer-ous . . . marinas, the central lodge complex has a theater, a deli, a . . . bowling alley, a game room, a world-renowned spa, and two restaurants. During the winter, it offers ice skating and an indoor-outdoor pool.'" Henrico leveled his insect eyes on us.

"Is that where you might work?" Louise asked.

He nodded.

She said, "I like ice skating."

Henrico told her, "If we go, all of the entertainment is free."

My mom asked me and Fulton, "What do you guys think?"

Fulton answered, "Missouri! Who's ever heard of anything cool there?"

I rubbed Punchy, who Henrico hadn't drowned in a bag yet.

She said, "The added benefit with Missouri is that The Lodge by the Lake will let us live in employee housing and supply us with free groceries from the commissary."

Louise raised her eyes. "What's a commissary?"

"It's the warehouse where they store food for their restaurants."

Fulton frowned. "It's pathetic that we've got to get free food and a free house."

"It is," my mom agreed flatly, "but we're broke. There's absolutely no money left. We need to rebuild."

"But Missouri!" Fulton moaned and glanced at me, hoping I'd say something bad about it.

"Whatever," I muttered.

"Say something, Cay. Say something bad about it, too. Don't be such a wimp!"

Me and Punchy went upstairs and looked at my lampshade, which, when I see it now, isn't interesting. It's white and dirty from dust. That's all. I can't figure out why I looked at it for so long, but I sat there 'til nighttime.

As usual, we moved during the worst weather. There was a monsoon, which is where water comes down so hard you can't see across your yard to the moving truck.

Everything we owned got wet when it was carried out to the Mayflower truck that was green and had a yellow sailing ship painted on the side. The logo and bad weather caused me to imagine our furniture sailing to the Midwest. But it didn't and couldn't. In fact, in the next few months we learned to hate the ship logo and the company for being idiots and driving most of our furniture to Abilene, Texas before losing it.

For a while, I stood outside watching the men load our things, then I turned and went into the house.

Because I had been staring at a boat and my dad had one, I thought about him and felt bad for how we'd be so far away. To feel better, I wandered into the kitchen and phoned him collect at his office. The weekend before, he had taken me, Fulton, and Louise up to Richmond, where we'd gone to museums and stayed in a nice hotel room. It had been fun, like we were in a popular television show about a happy family. For two straight days, he had been sad and loving and himself.

He answered, "Yeah?"

"Hey, Dad."

"Greetings, Cay. Why, might I ask, are you calling?"

"'Cause we're leaving in a little while."

"You trying to rub it in?"

"No, sir. I'm . . . "

"Well, you're doing it."

"It's just that I'm missing you, and . . . "

"Really, well, son, I believe I'm the one who should be missing people, don't you? You won't be alone, but that's how I'm going to be." He breathed deep.

"Sorry."

"Sorry doesn't cut it. It can't."

"Yes, sir."

"Have a good trip."

"Yes, sir."

"I'll see you in the next few years, maybe. Maybe never again."

"Yes, sir."

He hung up, and I walked into the living room. Our small television had been dumped crookedly on a built-in bookshelf, and I sat down on the bare floor next to Fulton and Louise and watched a double episode of *CHIPS*, starring California Highway Patrol officers who scuba dive, hang glide, and race dune buggies through deserts in their spare time.

When the second show was over, a mover came in and unplugged the television. He covered it with a plastic bag and carried it into the rain. The only thing left in our house was us, our travel bags, and some puddles on the floor.

Shortly, Henrico, looking as if he'd gone swimming in his clothes, came from the kitchen and growled, "We got to go, now."

So, just like that, we left Norfolk, the three old lady babysitters, Buddy, El Taste de Europa, Fulton's bad friends, and my life as a drunken kid without hope.

Through the monsoon, Henrico drove us all of the way to Charlottesville, Virginia, where we snuck Punchy, hidden in a canvas bag, into a hotel. Then Henrico went out and got hamburgers for everyone. When he got back, Mom and him went into their room, and me, Fulton, and Louise went into ours. The three of us watched a comedy show that seemed not so funny.

After a while, Fulton kicked the bed. "I can't believe we left Norfolk. We're gone."

Louise looked at him. "Should we call Dad?"

I told her, "I talked to him. He's a little mad at us for leaving."

Fulton laughed. "Mad at us?"

"He thinks we're abandoning him."

"We don't have a choice."

"But he thinks we have one."

"He knows we don't."

Louise said, "Maybe he's confused."

Fulton told her, "He's not confused, he's just being Dad."

The drive took two more days. The next day, in silence, we rumbled through the remainder of Virginia and over the West Virginia mountains. By late afternoon, we were deep in Kentucky and all that driving had gotten me and Louise antsy. We started bickering and couldn't quit. We nagged back and forth for a while, 'til I said, "Louise, don't poke me."

"You're the one poking."

"It's 'cause you touched Punchy's tail."

"I can touch Punchy's tail."

"Not when she's . . ."

Suddenly, as he drove, Henrico tried to grab us. It was a strange thing to see, his free hand reaching back like a crab claw, the three of us dodging it 'til my mom got him under control even though she seemed bored with all of us.

Seizing his arm, she said, "Calm down, Henrico."

"You tell them to calm down!"

"Fine. Calm down, kids," she said.

When all was quiet again, Louise whispered, "Henrico, sorry we made you mad."

He glanced over his shoulder. "When I say shut up, shut up! Do you understand?"

"Yes," she mumbled, and looked out the window.

Tired-sounding, my mom said, "Henrico, please be nice."

I put my head down and tried to think of a place I'd rather be but couldn't. Nothing seemed better or worse than where I was, which made no sense seeing as how anything should've been better than where I was.

At the end of the day, we stayed in a hotel across the street from a waffle house with a neon cowboy sign. That's where me and Fulton and Louise got pancakes for dinner. It was all right 'til we went back to our motel room and discovered how Punchy had pissed all over the floor so that the rug by the bathroom was squishy and stunk.

"I hate that dog," Henrico hissed.

I touched the wetness and said, "She's nervous."

Henrico didn't care.

To protect her, I pulled Punchy close.

In the morning, without telling the hotel about Punchy's pissing, we snuck out.

By noon, we passed over the Missouri River, curving around the bottom of the Gateway Arch. For some reason, I'd thought it was constructed out of gold, but it wasn't. From there, we traveled into the burned and rusty countryside of Missouri, where the landscape began to look like a black-and-white snapshot picture.

At six o'clock in the evening, we arrived at The Lodge by the Lake. Leaving Punchy in the car, the five of us went inside. While Henrico got us our rooms, we sat around a sunken fireplace in the middle of the lobby. Everything was polished, rough stone or wood. It was really upscale.

"It's nice," Fulton admitted.

Louise said, "I like it."

I nodded.

We had no idea.

The Middle of Nowhere

While our employee housing was getting tidied, we stayed in two Lodge by the Lake hotel rooms that were nice. In fact, they had to be about two hundred times nicer than the Sandy Gulf Motel, which we lived in when we first arrived in Florida. But what's funny is how when I consider the two places, I'd pick to stay in the Sandy Gulf Motel every time.

In Missouri, right away, Punchy, who we had to keep in a brown corrugated box so that she wouldn't pee around the room, started howling, and a man at the front desk called and told us to muzzle her. Fulton didn't know how, so he phoned my mom's and Henrico's room, and Henrico came and did it with a shoelace.

For the first few days we were there, me, Fulton, and Louise spent our time watching a lot of television, especially *Star Trek*. We also went bowling, ate food at the restaurants, and swam in the cold indoor/outdoor pool, where to go from inside to outside you ducked under a wall and went down and through an opening and came up opposite from where you started.

At first, it felt like a vacation. We didn't unpack. We didn't organize boxes or clean. We didn't go to a grocery store. All we did was explore the hotel. Then, about halfway through the week, my mom escorted me, Fulton, and Louise to the car, and the four of us headed for town to register for school.

"I'm gonna drop out," Fulton told her on the way. "I'll hitchhike back to Norfolk."

"Fine," she said.

We rumbled and rumbled down the twisty road forever, and I asked, "Do we have to go this far every day?"

"I think."

Fulton said, "Are you going to take us?"

"Nope. A bus stops in front of Blackhead."

Blackhead, in case you're confused, is the name of a type of zit but was also the name of the community we were moving into. For some reason, the people who started it thought Blackhead was upper class sounding. Maybe they'd never seen how one looks on your face, or maybe they were just stupid, I don't know. But the name of our new community was Blackhead, and I thought that was a bad sign.

When we got into the town of Lake of the Ozarks, the place wasn't actually there. All we saw were some closed down trinket and vacation shops that had once been houses, and the elementary school, where my mom enrolled Louise by talking to a lady with thirteen—I counted—big, fuzzy moles on her face. Afterward, Louise was nearly in tears for having to go there, so I said, "It'll be okay." I actually felt sorry for her, right up until we arrived at mine and Fulton's school.

It was fifty times worse.

If me and Fulton could've picked between a Grim Reaper-ish ghost jabbing a hand through our chests or going to class in that building, we would've picked the Grim Reaper ghost. I'm not exaggerating. The Lake of the Ozarks Upper School stood three stories high and reminded me of the Dark Ages, of poor people, and of being sick. It was constructed of mud, wood, and crumbly stones. Behind it, seeming out of place, was a brick smokestack that shot a hundred feet into the air, scraping the low Missouri clouds and spewing black exhaust.

The four of us stared before we undid our seatbelts like robots. Swallowing, my throat was thick and clogged with nerves.

Distantly, Fulton said, "It's not nice."

My mom told him, "It's Tudor style. It's popular in Europe, but I'm not sure it works well in Missouri." She got out, and the three of us followed her toward the front doors.

Inside, the hallways and classrooms were so dim the principal must have hated seeing where to go or something, because you couldn't. It was so dark you bumped into things. Still, the gloomy shadowiness wasn't as bad as the smell from the cafeteria. That odor, whatever it was, jabbed your nostrils like a wire bottlebrush.

Fulton looked around. "I can't stand this place."

Louise asked, "Why's it so dark?"

I stumbled along behind them, dizzy from the overwhelming stink. I even wished we were back in Norfolk and closed my eyes and wondered if I was suffering from a drunken nightmare. But, as we got closer and closer to the cafeteria, I knew I wasn't and wished, even harder, I was.

In the office, the principal shook each of our hands. Whenever he moved, the smell of burnt butter filled the room, causing my face to cringe. For some reason, at the end of his arms, his shirt cuffs were stained yellow, and I wondered if that's where the butter smell was coming from.

"So you're city boys?" he said to Fulton and me. His voice was strange and flat with a southern drawl showing up every few words.

"Not so much," I answered when Fulton didn't speak.

"I'm sure you'll get a comparable education here. I have no doubt. We're proud of our school."

I nodded.

"Here at Lake of the Ozarks Upper, we like to think of ourselves as family, like step-parents or guardians. We like to think that we are an integral part of your young lives."

"Okay," I said, but, for me, being like step-parents sounded bad.

He fetched some forms for my mom to fill out, which she did using a short, chewed-on pencil the secretary let her borrow. As she wrote, she explained that we'd be starting the upcoming Monday.

"See you bright and early," the principal said.

By the time we got outside, Fulton hadn't mumbled a single word for about an hour, so my mom said, "Fulton, talk?"

He looked at her and kicked the ground so that mud sprayed up. "Everything—everything in there makes me want to throw up! I want to puke right here!"

"It's different is all. It's not so bad."

Fulton leaned against one of the car doors and made a fist. "Come on, Mom, you know you're lying. You know it. It's not different, it's crap."

"Please, Fulton," she said, and, trying to calm his nerves, she drove us for a treat to The Lake of the Ozarks commercial strip. Unfortunately, we'd already found it since it was beside the elementary school, so she quit looking and we started back.

Forty minutes later, we walked into The Lodge by the Lake's fancy lobby, where I sat in front of the round fireplace and wondered what to do. I adjusted my butt and wondered and adjusted my butt some more. I imagined a hunter accidentally shooting one of his kneecaps off. It was a pretty terrible mistake to make, the kind my dad would get annoyed with. But I felt like we'd done something like that. We'd shot our kneecaps off in the middle of nowhere.

After a week in The Lodge by the Lake, we moved into our employee housing, which was a dump.

The basement was where me and Fulton were supposed to sleep and it was cold and empty and covered in orange shaggy carpeting that smelled like mildew and dirt, like they'd unrolled it over the forest floor and not on a slab of concrete. Also, the walls were covered with gloomy brown wood paneling that popped off and fell on you.

Because there were only three bedrooms, Fulton actually stayed in the television room. He took a corner alongside a big picture window and hung blankets along a string to block his bed from the rest of the room.

I got the bedroom in the way downstairs back, behind the utility room and past the back door. It was square-shaped and had curling paper tiles on the ceiling and the same orange carpet on the floor. A huge window identical to Fulton's looked out into the hillbilly woods.

In the downstairs bathroom, the panel walls were warped and the toilet rocked back and forth like a chair made for rocking. Around it, the carpet stayed wet with leaking sewer water. The dark shower was spotted with mildew and, instead of having a grate over the drain, there was a hole in the floor that if you weren't cautious you could fall in up to your knee. If your legs were really skinny, like Louise's, you might go all the way to your crotch.

At the top of the basement stairs was a narrow hallway. My mom and Henrico's bedroom was off to the right, facing out the front of the house and toward the road. Louise's was beside theirs, but it was in back, looking out over the lake. The three of them shared a tiny bathroom with a bouncy floor and a shower with a grate.

Off to the left of the steps was the main part of the house, including the kitchen that was crowded with busted shelves and cabinets. The dining and living rooms were connected. Both had gray painted walls, like a Navy ship, and different types of gold shag carpeting. At the far end of the living room, was the front door. In the wall blocking the kitchen from the living room was the fireplace that, for the first few weeks, we used like a television.

A few days after we moved in, it started to snow, but we still had to go to school. All day the snow came down. When me, Fulton, and Louise got home, a Mayflower moving truck was in front of the house, and a bunch of guys who looked like country-rock singers were unloading boxes, slipping and sliding down the slick steps to our door.

Me and Fulton and Louise went in and watched from the front window. We were staring out in a hypnotized way while the men struggled down the steps with a big piano.

My mom, who was organizing things in the house, came out and looked at it. "Whose is that?" she asked.

"Yours," a guy answered.

"We don't own a piano."

"Must."

"We don't."

Fulton went out the door and stood beside her. "It's true. We don't."

"Well, whose is it?" the guy asked them.

My mom said, "Not ours."

Four of the movers balanced the piano on a step and the driver went and got his clipboard. He came back. "This is your stuff," he confirmed, shaking his head like we were so stupid we couldn't recollect owning a piano.

"But that's really not ours," she told him.

The driver swatted the snow off his long hair. He scratched at the corner of his mouth and raised his eyebrows. "Ah, ma'am, you opened any of the boxes yet?"

"No."

"Why don't you go do that to see if anything's familiar."

My mom went down the steps and into the house. A few minutes later, she came out. "None of it belongs to us."

"Goddamn it!" the driver said. "Hold on! Hold on!" Turning, he stormed back up to the truck, got in, and started screaming on his CB radio. Two inches of snow accumulated on the blanket overtop the piano before he came back. "Your stuff must be lost."

She said, "What?"

"Lost. Lost loads are usually found within two to three weeks, so it's no big deal. Was probably sent to where this stuff was supposed to go."

"Two to three weeks?"

"Yeah."

"But we don't have any furniture, not even a chair."

"Nothing I can do."

My mom stared at him.

He laughed. "Welcome to Misery, ma'am. It's short for Missouri."

It seemed like more of a description.

In a Movie

In Missouri, on school days, we got off the bus nearly crazy from how other students thought our accents were English even though, to us, we sounded normal. As a matter of fact, on the first day I started at Lake of the Ozarks Upper, a boy said, "Caley, we all think you're from England."

"I'm not."

"Your voice sounds snobby. Did you know that?"

"I didn't. Sorry."

In fact, about two weeks after we started, I went into the bathroom and a huge kid named Kaiser, who smelled like cows, came from out of the dark and said, "Hey, new boy, you think you're something special, don't ya? Ya think you're like James Bond, huh?"

I shot my eyes down to where my worn shoes would be if I could've seen them in the zero light. "I don't."

"So then, if you ain't, come pee in the sink like me."

"In the sink? Um, that's all right." I looked toward where the sinks should be and could barely see their white porcelain. I told myself never to wash my hands at school again. "Thanks, though."

"Thanks? That what you're saying to me? Thanks! You're a prissy boy, huh?" He shoved me, and, normally, I would've thrown an elbow at him, but I didn't. I just let him push. "Prissy boy. Won't pee in the sink."

Feeling embarrassed, I left from the bathroom.

That afternoon, after we got home to our empty house, Fulton exploded at Mom for telling him to try to get along with his new classmates. "I'd like to, sure! I mean, I try to sound as ignorant as them, but I can't. I just can't! Sorry."

"They're not 'ignorant,' Fulton."

"You don't know. They actually think we're from England!"

Louise said, "I hate riding the bus for almost an hour. It makes my stomach feel gushy."

My mom leaned against the kitchen counter. "There's nowhere else, guys.

There's no other school, so get used to it."

Disappointed, the three of us, like always, headed out the door for the lodge and the deli with its bowling alley and the spa that was run by a Mexican man named Tony, who looked like a cartoon.

Stomping along the gravelly Blackhead streets, we cut through the woods and went along the golf course. That's how we avoided walking beside HH, which is the name of the big roadway that goes from the lodge all the way to town. It's not HH Street or Highway or Interstate, or anything, either. It's just HH. That's the type of thing they do in Missouri. They name things stupidly.

Walking the golf course took about a half hour, and Fulton was getting tired of it, so he said, "When we come back, let's find a shorter short cut."

I shrugged. I was a little nervous about exploring.

Around us, the grass was brown and flowed away, dipping toward a ravine on my left and rising to HH on the right. Off in the distance, trees were leafless and gray, matching the sky. Inside, I felt spongy, like I was dissolving from a person into a blob, which I was sort of doing due to eating so much free food at the deli.

"Fulton?" I said.

"Yeah?"

"Have you talked to Dad in a long time?"

"Nope."

"He told me not to call, but you think we should?"

Louise said, "Maybe he doesn't have our phone number?"

"We told him he could call the lodge," Fulton said, wiping his nose. "We told him that."

"He might've forgot."

"He didn't forget."

Louise fidgeted with her gloves. "Do you think, if we call him on the phone, we'll have to do it collect?"

"Maybe," I answered, wondering if Mom and Henrico would pay for long distance phone bills.

Fulton asked, "When has Henrico ever given us anything, especially for Dad?"

Louise said, "Never."

"So you answered your own question."

When we got to the Lodge, we went down to the deli and the bowling alley and sat at a table. Bored, I got up and got a deli sandwich and a piece of carrot cake. When I was finished, I went and got a Firewater Cream Soda and a bag of potato chips to go with a candy bar.

Fulton said, "Stop eating so much, Caley."

"I'm not."

"You are." He went and registered for a bowling lane. We put on shoes and played. I wanted to do something else, but there wasn't anything except the spa and a few coin games. It turned out that the ice skating rink was just a small frozen pool that they had to close whenever it snowed, which was all of the time.

Eventually, Louise said, "I hate bowling, I decided. I want to swim."

"Go swim then," Fulton snapped.

"Not alone."

"I'm not freezing my behind in there."

"I'll go," I said, glad not to bowl.

So we went over to the spa and past Tony, the spa manager, who was also a body builder who went around without a shirt while wearing the tiniest pair of swim trunks. He also kept the whirlpool water near to boiling and the indoor/outdoor pool a half-degree above freezing, explaining it was how professional spas ran their water. We always complained, though, so that Tony started getting a look on his face like he really did want to freeze or boil us.

I changed in the men's room and met Louise out by the pool.

"You jump in first," she said.

"No thanks."

She got down on her knees and pulled a floating volleyball over. "We can throw this back and forth and whoever drops it has to jump in."

I shrugged.

We threw for about twenty minutes 'til Tony said, "No balls on the deck!"

Shivering from jumping into the ice-water pool, me and Louise rushed to get warm in the hot tub area, except the water was too scorching to stick even one leg in. I whispered to Louise, "Tony says no balls, but he walks around with his hanging out of his tiny swimming suit."

She smiled. "You mean like his penis balls?"

"Yeah."

She laughed.

"That's like the smallest bathing suit in the world."

"It might fit Snoopy," she said. She tried to dunk her leg up to her knee. "Wish he'd turn the temperature down."

"Maybe he likes boiling his balls for dinner?"

"Like on the stove?" she asked, surprised.

"In here, Louise." I pointed to the whirlpool, where my foot was just barely beneath the surface and looking like a noodle.

Fulton spent the rest of the afternoon playing pinball across from the theater that was showing a redneck Burt Reynolds movie. The box office didn't open 'til seven, so nobody was around.

It took me and Louise a half hour to find him, and, when we did, he smiled and said, "Watch this, guys." He kicked the pinball machine's coin box. Two games popped up. "It's free this way," he told us, and went around and kicked two other machines so that they gave him free games.

We played for about an hour, but it wasn't any fun. I never liked pinball.

Leaving out a side door for home, Fulton stopped. "Let's cut through the woods. If we go that way, it should take us down into the ravine then up to Blackhead."

I stared along the rocky lane that led past the lodge's cheaper rooms. "It might not connect with Blackhead. You don't know."

"But it might."

"It's getting late."

"So."

"What if there's a stream down there and we fall in?"

"Don't be a wuss."

Louise said, "I'll go."

I rested my hands in my coat pockets. "I'm not saying I don't wanna. It's just, I was thinking of Louise. If she wants to, I will."

Fulton said, "She already said she wants to."

"Fine," I told them.

Together, we started down the rocky road, past the overflow parking lots and down to a sign that said, LODGE EMPLOYEES ONLY. Fulton tossed a rock at it, and we went through a shabby trailer park for hotel workers. A scary-looking waiter sat out on the steps of a trailer. Wearing a big winter jacket, he smoked a cigarette. We waved, and he waved back.

We walked past the trailer park and into the woods. We went into a deep hollow of ground that arrived at a little creek you could jump over without hardly any effort, even Louise.

It was getting dark and the Missouri woods were feeling eerie and unfriendly to me. Around us, the trees seemed fake and made of metal. Each looked gray and rusting so that I wondered if we weren't really outside but were in a movie that was supposed to appear to be the Missouri woods. I thought I might be an actor who forgot I was acting and all of our bad luck—from the burps to living in Missouri—was a script.

We started up the far side of the hill, and I tried to spot cameramen but couldn't find any. Breathing hard, I said, "Are we in a movie?"

Fulton answered, "No!"

"You know how it sometimes feels like you are?"

Louise said, "Yeah."

Fulton said, "Sounds like something insane people ask."

Nervous, I turned and kept walking, pushing aside shrubs and bramble 'til I became terrified that we were lost forever in the lumpy hills surrounding the lake. When we came out on a rocky road with houses across the street, it was almost solid darkness.

"This is Blackhead," Fulton told us.

"How do you know?" Louise looked at him, shivering.

"By how ugly it is and because I recognize that house from walking with Mom." He checked his watch. "It took us twenty minutes. It's half as far that way."

I didn't trust him. "Seemed longer."

"It's because the whole way you were about to go to the bathroom in your pants."

"Was not."

"You were, Cay. You're always scared."

"I'm not," I told him.

Fulton scoffed. He turned and me and Louise followed behind him up the road and to the steps down to our employee house, where we went inside and watched the fireplace and ate chicken strips and squash.

Later, when I went downstairs to get a schoolbook, Punchy started growling at the bathroom door. Curious, I flicked on the dim light and found a huge rat slinking about on the wet rug around the toilet. Screaming, I called for my mom and Fulton and Louise. They arrived just in time to see Punchy attack the rat around the neck like a lion on a gazelle. That rodent didn't have a chance.

When it was dead, my mom said, "I guess it came in through the shower drain."

"Yeah," Fulton agreed.

Of course, in the night it was hard to sleep in my room that was tucked in the far back corner of the house and had a huge window. I kept having to pee but was scared of going to the bathroom because I might step on a rat, get bitten, and die of rabies. I also kept looking out the picture window for cameramen filming me, but I couldn't find them. I looked 'til about five in the morning, my brain feeling trembley and slow to understand things.

A Massive Wussy

Me, Fulton, and Louise let another week go by before we took the phone from off its hook and dialed my dad's house. Holding the receiver, I felt like I was about to drink poison or slam my fingers in a door, because I knew how the conversation would go, especially when Kora answered and the operator asked if she accepted the charges for my collect call. "Charges? My God!"

"Does that mean you don't accept them, ma'am?" the operator asked.

Kora hesitated then spat, "No. I accept."

Around me, the kitchen and dining area seemed to be turning in wide circles. Nervous, I said, "Hey, Kora."

She said back, "I'll get your dad."

"Okay."

I waited, wondering how he'd act. I didn't expect he'd be happy, but I wasn't sure.

Snatching up the phone, he said, "Cay, been quite a long time, am I right?"

"Yes, sir."

"Having too much fun to phone?"

"No. It's just . . . you told me not to."

"I believe you understood precisely what I meant.'"

"I didn't."

He replied, "Let's expedite this little briefing, why don't we? What can I help you with, young man?"

He was in his army personality, which is one of my least favorite ways he can be. When he's army, his voice is cold and harsh. "Ah . . . well, nothing. Me, Fulton, and Louise just wanted to talk."

"Really? That's odd."

"Do—do you think?"

"Let's see. Since you shipped out, private, I haven't gotten one call or letter. Nothing. It has been the most devastating experience of my life. So, yes, I find it odd."

"Sorry."

"You are never sorry, son. I have learned that about you. No matter, give me the recon on your transfer."

"What?"

"Missouri, recruit, how is it?"

"It's—it's not so nice."

"What do you want from me?"

"Nothing, sir."

"Your unit hasn't made any attempt to contact me."

"I know, sir."

"No you don't."

"Dad, we didn't want to move. We wanted to stay in Norfolk and Yorktown."

"Horsecrap!"

My gut rumbled like I'd eaten pizza or ice cream twenty minutes before. "We did. Anyway, Dad, if ever you want, you can write or call us. If you want, you always can. We'd like that."

"Son, let me give you a little declassified information. I am old school, if you know what that means. Where I'm from, officers don't coddle enlisted men. It's the other way around. You write me, and I'll write you. But I don't get a letter, you don't get a letter. Understand?"

"Yeah."

"How 'bout a 'Yes, sir,' boy?"

"Yes, sir."

"That all you want to say?"

I tried to remember what I'd been planning to blabber about but nothing came to mind. "I guess."

"Then put your brother or sister on."

I handed Louise the phone so that his military self could blow her to pieces, then I went downstairs to the dirt-smelling basement and back to my room, where I sat on the floor alongside my cot, which was one of the five cots we were borrowing 'til our furniture arrived.

For some reason, I started having a hard time breathing and looked at the ceiling to stretch my throat out. Staring at the stained tiles, a tear dragged down from an eyeball, and I pounced on it with a hand. "How can you be how you are?" I asked myself. "Why're you so bad?" I banged a fist against my head. "Why?"

A few minutes passed, and I slapped my cheek. Breathing as heavy as Darth Vader, I stood and left my room to talk with Louise.

She was sitting on her cot, her face tracked with tears.

I stumbled in and garbled, "He wasn't so nice, huh?"

She picked at the fuzz on her blanket. "Cay, he misses me. He's gonna send me a bracelet."

My breathing got harder. "Nah-ah."

"Nah-ah, what?"

"He—he wasn't acting friendly."

"He was."

I glared at her in disbelief. "Where's Fulton?"

"Still on the phone," she whispered, hugging her pillow.

I walked toward the kitchen and stopped before I got there. Fulton was saying, "They're such grits. Some don't even brush their hair or teeth. I mean, their faces even have dirt on them . . ."

My dad must have replied, because Fulton told him, "It's bad."

When he finally hung up the phone, I stepped into the kitchen.

He looked at me.

I said, "Why . . . was he nice to you?"

Fulton shrugged. "Who knows?"

"He wasn't to me."

Fulton raised his eyebrows. "I didn't think he would be to me, but he was."

I prodded the outside of my neck, scared that I wouldn't be able to breathe in a few minutes. "Why do you think he did that?"

"What?"

"Why do you think he was mean to me and nice to you and Louise?"

"You know Dad," Fulton said. "You can't ever predict why he's doing things." He squinted. "What's wrong? You're breathing like you got a pillow over your face."

I shook my head. "Nothing's wrong but that I think my throat's shrinking down and strangling me."

"Open your mouth."

I did.

He looked down it. "Cay, you jerk, it's just as big as normal, so stop."

The next day, after school, we took our shortcut down into the ravine and up through the muddy trailer park. Entering The Lodge by the Lake's swinging side doors, we went into the gift shop.

Fulton looked over some books, and Louise squeezed some stuffed animals wearing sweatshirts. She told Fulton, "I wish I had one of these."

He rolled his eyes. "They're stupid, Louise."

I picked my dad the ugliest postcard I could find, hoping to show him the area. It had a picture of a sailboat drifting on the lake at sunset. As bad as it was, though, it wasn't as bad as Missouri actually was. I figured the gift shop wasn't allowed to sell realistic, gloomy postcards of the state, but they should've at least had one.

I went to the counter, and the lady said, "This all?"

I nodded and reached for the change in my pocket. Fishing around, I began to wonder if she thought I'd stolen something. "I—I don't steal," I said. "If I did, I'd be stupid. My stepfather's the new chef."

She nodded. "Okay."

"I'm getting the postcard for my dad. He's mad we haven't written."

She said, "It costs a quarter."

I paid. "You want me to empty my pockets?"

She shook her head. "For what?"

"To see I didn't steal."

"I trust you."

But for some reason I emptied them anyway. "See."

She nodded.

Out in the hallway, Fulton said, "God, Cay, why don't you calm down or something."

"I want to," I told him, but felt so wound up my hands trembled.

We went down to the deli, like usual, and I got a fried fish sandwich, a hamburger, and a double wedge of chocolate cake. Eating, I wrote a note to my dad.

> Deer Dad,
> Here is a picture of the Lake of the Ozarks, but its not true. To be true, it would have to be ugly. If you look, theres nothing around on the shore but trees. Thats true. Fulton and I wish there were bears around. Louise is mad that the ice skating rink is just a pool. We all 3 hate school. This kid name Kiser pees in the sinks. Henrico says the restaurant kitchen is nice. Mom wants to get a job because she doesn't know anybody. There's a Japanese man here who does art that looks Chinese. He sells it to torists. There aren't any this time of year. I wish you could see it. Its horrible.
> Love, Cay

Fulton said, "Maybe you shouldn't eat all that cake, Cay?"

"Why not?" I asked, tucking the postcard into a coat pocket. "It tastes good."

Louise, who was having some candy said, "Gross! When you smell in this bag, it smells like feet."

She tilted the bag over and I sniffed. "It does."

Louise said, "You wanna smell, Fulton?"

"Of course I don't," he told her, getting up. He jammed his hands in his coat pockets and walked off between the tables, stopping at the jukebox just as Stacy, the daughter of the The Lodge by the Lake's manager, walked in with her boyfriend, a football player with a black Trans Am that screeched up smoking rubber whenever he left with her for anywhere.

Fulton gawked at her.

I did, too.

In the entire state, Stacy was probably the only fox. She was so cute I couldn't talk when, during good weather, she waited outside with us at the bus stop in the morning. In fact, all of the grit boys at Lake of the Ozarks Upper were in love with her, and she knew it.

Stacy and Rob walked right past Fulton like he wasn't there. Holding hands, they sat at a table beside the spa's entrance.

Fulton stared after them. He left the jukebox and trudged back over to me and Louise. Leaning, he said, "She didn't even look at me, and I'm older than her. I'm actually older."

"Yeah, I guess she gets to ignore you."

"No, she doesn't, Cay."

My head felt stuffed deep in a box full of nose tissues. It was hard to say, but I explained to him, "Fulton, all of us look worse than her."

"You're the one who looks worse. I look like always."

I blinked, surprised by what he'd said. "I look like always, too."

"No, you don't. You're eating too much."

"Like about two lunches a day," Louise agreed, and offered me a piece of feet-smelling candy.

I popped one in my mouth and glanced down at the two empty Styrofoam plates that were slathered with grease. I looked at what remained of the double slice of cake I'd eaten most of. "It's 'cause it's free and there's nothing else to do."

Fulton twisted around and studied Stacy, who was holding Rob's hand. He said, "There's other stuff than eating."

"But our television hasn't arrived yet."

"There're things outside."

"Like what?" I asked, unable to think.

"Like going and looking and finding something. I don't know. You're such a massive wussy these days, you don't look."

Hands trembling, I said, "I'm not a wussy."

At that, Fulton laughed.

An Unhooking Sound

For the second year in a row, Thanksgiving wasn't traditional. Where me, Fulton, and Louise had spent the previous untraditional Thanksgiving with Mrs. Morto and her leaky bladder that got the back of her dress wet sometimes, in Missouri my mom ate with us. Still, we didn't have a table or chairs or even anything to cook with yet, so we went to The Lodge by the Lake and played like hotel guests.

Pulling into the parking lot out front, my mom said, "Isn't this going to be nice?"

Louise asked, "Do we have to eat turkey?"

"You can get anything you want."

Fulton told her, "If you don't get turkey, Louise, it's not Thanksgiving, it's just a regular meal."

We passed through the lobby and around the circular fireplace. We waited at the entrance to The Tupelo Room, where Henrico was the chef. It was The Lodge by the Lake's best restaurant.

When the maître d' came to seat us, me, Fulton, and Louise recognized him from the trailer park, where he smoked cigarettes on the steps of a double-wide trailer that slumped in the middle. He said, "Follow me, please," and led us to a table beside a large window overlooking the ice skating pool that was closed due to snow and fluctuating weather conditions.

The four of us inspected our Tupelo Room menus.

My mom said, "It is so sad that Henrico has to work today."

I didn't feel that way. In fact, it was because he was gone that I felt thankful about something.

Fulton inspected the wine list. "Mom, can I have a beer?"

"No."

"It's not like I never had one."

"I'm aware of that, Fulton."

He rolled his eyes at me, and I could tell he thought it was a joke that my mom didn't know he'd had more than just a beer before. But it didn't seem funny to me. Instead of laughing, I felt guilty. To make that go away, I tried to say something silly about the skating rink, but my vocal cords were tightened up like guitar strings, and, instead of making words, they made a squeal like a cat squeals after you step on its tail.

Mom looked at me. "Cay? You okay, dear?"

Surprised, I answered, "Y—yeah."

She held her eyes on me for a second, then she forgot about it.

A waitress came and asked if we wanted refreshments.

My mom told her, "Three Cokes, and I'd like a bottle of the house red."

Fulton closed his menu and showed the lady the front. "Why's there a picture of Mississippi on the cover?"

"It's for how Tupelo is a town in Mississippi."

"Oh."

Mom unfolded her cloth napkin and asked, "Is the menu influenced by Tupelo's regional cuisine or something?"

The lady shook her head. "I don't know, ma'am. I think we got mostly European food. A guest told me Tupelo's only got rubber and plastic factories."

Fulton laughed.

My mom smiled pleasantly.

When the bread came, to relax I ate it all.

My greediness for the bread must've annoyed Fulton, because after a few minutes he held up the basket and said, "Thanks for sharing, Cay."

"We'll get more," my mom told him.

A short while later, Henrico made a big issue out of delivering our salads, which I could tell got all of the other guests jealous and thinking we were special. But it wasn't special to me since I was hoping not to see him 'til at least the next day. Also, he looked strange in his tall chef's hat. Also again, he kissed Mom on her cheek, leaving a little spit behind that made my stomach push the bread partway back up my throat. Straightening, he asked what each of us was having for dinner.

Worried that he wanted to sabotage our food with poison, I lied and said I was going to order a piece of fish instead of turkey.

Later, when I was done eating, I looked around to see if someone eating fish had died.

◆

Over the next few weeks, the temperature sunk to five degrees. Plus, it started snowing so that it got hard to walk to the lodge, especially because all we had on our feet were old low-cut sneakers and our ankles were exposed due to how our pants were three-year-old high waters.

We'd never seen so much snow. It didn't matter, though. They didn't close the idiotic schools.

From Monday to Friday, me, Fulton, and Louise trudged through foot-high drifts up to HH, feeling cheated. Back in Yorktown and Norfolk, if there'd been a half-inch of snow on the ground, schools shut down for fear of car accidents and kids slipping. It was a joke. But in Missouri, where driving was terrifying, it seemed like they never wanted to close. Even on terrible days, we'd stand alongside HH waiting for the bus. On the really cold mornings, foxy Stacy would sit in luxury beside us since her mother or father usually carried her to the bus stop in their huge, warm Suburban truck.

About that time, before I realized I'd already turned into a blob, I quit wearing my coat to school. I thought it made me look chubby. So I stood there looking like a retarded chubby kid in a thin shirt. All the while, I wished Stacy and her parents would invite me in from the cold. They must've considered us gross, though, because they never did and probably wouldn't have if we'd fainted and frozen against their front tires.

When the bus pulled up, Manfred Mann's "Blinded by the Light" song always floated out through the rubber crack in the entrance door. The driver, with his black bicycle racing gloves and dark airplane glasses, nodded to us as we boarded. He never spoke and just replayed "Blinded by the Light" over and over excluding if he got irritated at students for roughhousing. For that, he'd stop the bus and the music.

On HH, which is a swerving, hilly road that passes above deep ravines and cliffs that tumble down to the lake, the bus always skidded and veered, its tires losing their grip in the snow so that, I'm not kidding, we sometimes barreled down hills sideways, like a giant yellow plow. Luckily, the area was mostly desolate and nobody was ever coming.

After arriving at Lake of the Ozarks Upper, I'd sit in my various desks watching the snow accumulate like dandruff on the shoulders of a kid in math who needed Head and Shoulders treatment shampoo. All day I'd get more and more upset about not going home and how I was stuck stumbling from class to class through the dark hallways where everybody ran into each other and water fountains and garbage cans, too.

One afternoon, in PE, I hated everything so much that I refused to play dodgeball. The whistle blew, and I just stood like a totem pole and allowed myself to be pummeled. After that happened for the fifth time, the coach came over and said, "Caley, I have noticed that you ain't trying to be your best."

I nodded. "Yes, sir, I know."

"Why not?"

"'Cause . . . I don't dodge well."

"Don't make no difference. I grade you on your participation. You gotta try."

"They all wanna hit me first anyway. So I let them."

He roughed up my hair. "Son, that's probably because you act so snotty. Know what I mean?"

I figured he meant my accent.

"I got a suggestion. Why don't you try to talk American and play hard instead of surrendering? That might earn you a little respect from your peers. What'cha think of that?"

I said, "Yes, sir."

He grinned. "Well, good."

That afternoon, rumbling through a crushing snowfall, the bus ride to

Blackhead took more than two hours.

When me, Fulton, and Louise finally got off, we all had to pee so badly we hurried down the road. A minute later, Stacy's parents' Suburban sped past us, spraying snow on Fulton. "God, they're douche bags," he said.

Turning the corner to our road, we plowed straight to our employee-housing home and went inside. Dropping our bags in the front area, the three of us started for the bathrooms but stopped short to stare into the living room area. Our couch and coffee table were situated together with nothing else around them.

We walked into the kitchen and found a few familiar dishes on the counter and my mom's old kettle on the stove.

In the dining room, three chairs were lined up against the window, but the table was missing.

"Mom!" Fulton called.

Mom came out from her bedroom. "Yes?"

"Everything arrived?" he asked hopefully.

She shrugged. "Some things. They found one of our crates in Texas. They're still looking for the other three."

I leaned forward. "Anything from my room?"

"A box."

"Mine?" Fulton wanted to know.

"Nothing. But almost all of Louise's room arrived."

Louise jumped in the air. "Yeah!"

Fulton slammed his books on the counter and went downstairs to use the toilet. A few seconds later, he was back. "The television's down there," he said brightly, finding, as usual, something to be glad about.

My mom nodded.

"Least that's good. I'm sick of looking at logs in the fire."

"Me, too," I seconded, trying to be more like Fulton.

Fulton said, "Hey, Cay, you wanna see what's on?"

I blinked. I wasn't sure and had to go to the bathroom so bad my stomach hurt.

Mom came over and placed a letter in my hand. "It's from your dad," she said in a nice way.

I told Fulton, "I gotta read this first," and walked like a zombie down to the rocky toilet. Afterward, I went to my room and stared out the big picture window and into the snowy sky. Tired of being nervous, I jammed my thumb under the flap of the letter and tore along the top. Inside was a card. It said:

> Dear Son,
> Thanks for writing. I will cherish your letter forever, for my hurt is so deep and impenetrable that any sign of you is a miracle. In short, my heart is broken and a void resides in my soul. I can only look forward to the day that I retire and relocate to Missouri, if upon my arrival you still remember your loving father. I say with absolute honesty that the meager happiness that survived when your mother divorced me has been stripped away. I am lost. Hence, because I have no need of money, I've enclosed twenty dollars for you to split three ways with your brother and sister.
>
> Inconsolable,
> Dad
>
> P.S. If I were there, I would help you learn to spell. Your spelling is atrocious. But, alas, I am far away and can only offer advice, thanks to your mother, from a million desperate miles.

I looked at my box from Texas. I couldn't open it. Considering how my dad felt, it seemed selfish to do something that might make me happy. So, deflating myself of any good feelings—which I didn't have many of anyway—I shuffled out to the main part of the basement, where Fulton was watching a soap opera.

"Fulton," I croaked, "I'm going to the lodge. You wanna come?"

"There's like a foot and a half of snow out there, bonehead. It's terrible."

"I know." I went upstairs and told my mom, "I'm going to the lodge."

"For what?"

"For a snack, I guess." I put on the coat that I thought made me look chubby and left out the door. The snow was deep enough so that it was hard to walk and soaked down into my already-wet sneakers so that in a split second my feet ached.

Passing over the hill and away from our house, I continued down the road to our shortcut through the woods. Without stopping, I stepped over the ditch and wandered between two creaky trees before pushing through heavy underbrush. Looking up, snow fell so hard I couldn't even see the tops of trees, as if they were haunted by the skirt of a ghost.

After a time, I arrived at a clearing where the snow seemed to be falling funny and perfectly straight. Bothered, I watched and listened, and the flakes hissed when they landed on the ground. Everything looked unfriendly and mean.

I rubbed my eyeballs and realized I was seeing X-rayish, like I had a few times in Norfolk. I stepped in a circle and the big wet trees looked made from enormous leg bones. Shivering, I yelled, "Stop!" like a total lunatic. Then, scared like I have never been in my entire life, scared like I was getting hunted by a English-person-hating hick carrying a deer rifle, I raced back to the road, where, jumping the small ditch, I slipped and slammed down like a hippo.

Breathing hard, I pushed myself to my knees and stood. Catching my breath, I stared at an empty house across the street. It looked like the sort of place that might be haunted, so I trotted all the way to our employee home, where I opened the door and headed downstairs to stand near Fulton and Louise, who, along with my mom, were watching television.

I said, "Hey."

Without turning, my mom said, "Thought you were going to the lodge?"

"Decided not to." I slunk behind them and leaned against the dark wood paneled wall. Sucking air, I touched the back of my head to it, and there was an unhooking sound. A second later, a sheet of wood paneling fell on me, scratching a perfect, straight line on my scalp.

Playing dramatic, I collapsed on my side and rolled over like I'd gotten hit by a bullet on a traditional battlefield instead of an untraditional and really ugly basement to an employee housing home.

My mom left the TV and looked at me.

"This—this is how things are now. It's like nothing's good and everything's bad," I rasped up at her.

She nodded gently, and for a few seconds I saw her worry and care the way she used to. Then her face shivered slightly, and I knew she was wrestling those feelings away. She moved the board, and said coldly, "Cay, sweetie, don't exaggerate. Okay? It only makes things worse."

Fulton told me, "Missouri sucks is why you feel that way. I feel it, too."

I squirmed and peered up at him. "Fulton, are—are you serious?"

"I can't stand this Goddamn dumpy place."

Louise told me, "Except that I have my furniture, I don't like living here, either."

I nodded. It was nice to know I wasn't alone. But getting hit by the wall seemed so absolutely unlucky that I thought my situation was worse than theirs. In my head, I even pictured their unluckiness like a pile of dirt and mine like a mountain.

Near-Death Experience

Over Christmas break, it continued snowing. I remember that like it left an ugly mark on a film strip of my memory. What I don't remember is any of my Christmas presents excluding two.

The first present I recall is my dad's. He gave me his old Kodak Instamatic camera that he sent without any film or a place to process film that wasn't seventy miles away. Unfortunately, along with his old, used camera came complaints that I didn't send any photos, even after I explained that in order to do that I'd have to develop them myself.

The second present I remember was from Fulton. He gave me a book called *The Hobbit*, which was white and didn't look so fascinating since there weren't any pictures inside. It came with complaining, too. A few minutes after I unwrapped it, Fulton started in on how I had to get reading. "It'll take your mind off of where you are," he promised. But that was impossible, I thought. My mind felt solidly caught.

A few hours later, I told him, "I looked through and saw it's got goblins in it."

"So?"

"So I don't like goblins."

"You're not supposed to, Cay."

"They're like devils."

"I know."

I stared at Fulton's face. "Reading about them might keep me awake," I explained, ignoring how I'd been suffering unbelievable insomnia since getting hit by the wall.

"Cay, the goblins make the book exciting."

But I didn't want devilish excitement. What I wanted was calmness.

But calmness is hard to find when you feel hysterical about not sleeping. And being hysterical at night is not a good way to get tired. And when you're overtired, it's hard to be calm. It was like a snake eating its tail from behind.

About a week into January, the heavy snowfall we'd been having was replaced by something worse. The first of six blizzards roared through the area, dumping so much snow it closed the state, and, finally, The Lake of the Ozarks school system. Excited, me, Fulton, and Louise whooped it up for finally getting the day off. We had no idea we'd miss thirty-three straight school days, a situation that sounds good but was like getting locked away for a crime you didn't commit.

Being snowbound in Blackhead, all we saw was each other and the lodge. All we talked to was each other and a few people at the lodge. All we did was the same thing. Every single day was like the day before, and the day before was long and so boring it made you feel like you were getting Chinese water torture treatment along with being a prisoner.

To keep us from going crazy, which wasn't working for me, Fulton developed a schedule. We started the day by watching something I can't remember on television. We'd do other things I can't remember, then wrap plastic bags around our sneakers and leave the house before noon. We'd trek through waist deep snow to the lodge, where we bowled, played pinball, swam, and gorged like starving kids. Daily, we left in time to arrive home by four o'clock, when *Star Trek* came on the religious channel. We had to see *Star Trek*.

One afternoon, however, we started back as the third blizzard of the year got going, which was a big mistake.

With the wind humming in our ears and our wet hair frozen like tree branches, we passed through the trailer park area. Bent and blinking, we couldn't see more than a few feet ahead, and, due to that, we took a wrong turn and shoved our way through the deep drifts 'til we arrived at an open area where a tree had recently toppled.

"Is this a field?" I bellowed over the wind.

Fulton yelled, "It's a frozen over cove of the lake."

"What?"

"It's an inlet of the lake! See how the tree's halfway underwater?"

Shivering wildly, I nodded. "I guess we gotta go back!"

Fulton hollered, "I'm not! I'm going across and up the other side! Blackhead's probably right there!" He pointed.

Nervous, I said, "Let's just turn around!"

"Yeah, Fulton!" Louise seconded.

Fulton shouted, "Don't be a bunch of wimps. The lake's been frozen forever, and, if we go back to the trailer park, we'll miss part of *Star Trek*!"

I looked down to where my thighs disappeared into the snow. I didn't want to miss *Star Trek*. For whatever reason, I was concerned that if I did, my grindingly numbing schedule would get shuffled improperly, which might trigger a panic attack or an avalanche of guilt for how I let everyone down by becoming such a loser. "Fine!" I said, shoving off for the frozen lake top. The snow was so deep that I jumped onto the fallen tree trunk since it only had a sprinkle of white powder on the top.

Fulton followed.

Louise stayed where she was, yelling that we were stupid.

The swirling gusts kept us off balance, so that we nearly tumbled from the tree about fifty times. We were about three-quarters of the way along, having completely forgotten about how Louise wouldn't survive in the woods alone, when there was a series of enormous popping sounds beneath us.

I looked over my shoulder at Fulton.

He said, "That wasn't the lake. The lake's been frozen for more than a month!"

Hesitant, I got down and straddled the trunk like it was a horse. Slowly, I slid forward 'til I noticed a strange hole in the snow alongside a big limb. Instantly, my stomach twisted up. Beneath a thick sheet of lake ice, where there should've been water, there wasn't any. In its place was a long drop to sharp, gray rocks.

Behind me, Fulton yelled, "Don't move!"

I didn't.

"They must've let out water from the dam!" he called in my ear.

"What?"

"They must've pumped water from the lake after it froze!"

Snowflakes pelted my cheeks. "We're overtop of air!"

"And rocks!"

A large hunk of ice broke loose from the side of the hole, dropping 'til it exploded somewhere far beneath us.

Fulton delicately turned around.

Heart thumping unsteadily, I did the same. Three large snaps shook the tree, and I winced.

Frightened, Fulton hopped up and ran the length of the trunk, diving for the shore like a superhero trying to fly. It wouldn't be the last time he'd abandon me in a bad situation.

Beneath me, the tree quaked some more, and I closed my eyes, sure that I was about to die. I waited and listened to Fulton and Louise yell for me over the wind. After a few minutes, I reopened my eyes, stood, and shuffled forward delicately.

It was strange. The plastic bags around my sneakers hadn't bothered me on the way out, but coming back they made my treads feel slippery and dangerous. A gust came, and I leaned into it. When it slackened, I lost my balance and fell face-first onto the hanging lake ice.

The cove and all of the snow built up on it shook.

Terrified, I paddled furiously through a deep drift, and finally slumped against the shore, where I nearly fainted, which maybe would've been nice since I was safe and what's fainting but kind of sleeping. And I needed to sleep.

Louise hollered, "I told you guys! I told you that you were being stupid!"

"Shut up!" Fulton answered back. "We almost died!"

"I told you!" she repeated.

Following our tracks back to the trailer park, we reorganized and went our normal shortcut up the hill to Blackhead. Along the way, I didn't think about almost dying. That didn't start 'til after *Star Trek*, which, tragically, we missed half of.

Before dinner, while I worried about what might happen for only seeing half of *Star Trek*, I remembered our near-death experience. It didn't upset me. If we'd gone down, I figured we would've proved to my mom that Missouri really did suck. If I'd died on the rocks, she would've seen that we weren't exaggerating.

What didn't occur to me was how, if I'd died, I couldn't have enjoyed my mom's new knowledge. That's a bad miscalculation, the sort that was starting to pass through my mind a lot.

A few days later, on the morning an eighteen-wheeler delivered a second crate of furniture and boxes, I realized something. Until moving to Missouri, I hadn't watched *Star Trek* every day. Aside from other things, it was the only difference I could think of in my life.

I considered that while the moving van finished unloading our stuff and rolled slowly up the hill to the corner. I thought about it on the way to the lodge and back. I thought about it 'til almost four o'clock in the afternoon, when Fulton said, "*Star Trek's* about on."

Straight away, a switch was thrown in my power-outaged brain. Instantly, I recognized something obvious that I hadn't seen before. Kirk and Spock and the old-style film coloration had a strange grip on me. Obviously, they were causing me my problems with sleeping and bad feelings, and I had to avoid them or I'd never feel good again.

I was starting to lose my mind.

Darth Vader and Chewbacca

Similar to every snowed-in afternoon, *Star Trek* was playing in the family room, making it impossible for me to leave my room, where I felt trapped like a squirrel in a squirrel cage. Having run out of things to do, I huddled into a corner that smelled like dog pee and picked up *The Hobbit*. I opened it and read the first few pages. I liked it well enough and kept reading. I read all of the way 'til dinner and didn't want to put the story down then.

It was early in February, and we'd been out of school for nearly four weeks. Having no homework and a big blank day allowed me to concentrate on my bad feelings, making it so that they had grown to be like a guillotine that was dangerous and dull so that if it dropped fast it would only cut your neck partially off, causing it to hurt so bad you'd wish it had done a better job.

The previous Saturday, I'd become so bothered after watching *Saturday Night Live* that I banned the show like I had *Star Trek*. No more John Belushi or Dan Aykroyd or Bill Murry. I didn't like how sarcastic those guys were about everything. I couldn't even stand to see a commercial starring them without feeling creepy.

At the lodge a few days later, while I ate a second lunch as Fulton and Louise bowled, Henrico suddenly showed up in the deli.

He looked at me like I disgusted him. "No wonder you're getting fat," he said. "Get your coat, we're driving to Eldon for supplies." He went over and told Fulton and Louise the same thing.

Fulton said, "Henrico, if we go now, we'll miss *Star Trek*."

Henrico looked like he might punch him. "Be in the lobby in a few minutes," he hissed.

Nervous, we grabbed our things and left to the lobby where we found our car idling beneath the huge wooden carport out front where visitors check in. Henrico was checking the chains on our tires. Satisfied, he squeezed his big body into the driver's seat, next to Mom.

Fulton asked, "Why're we going to Eldon?"

My mom said, "Because we're running out of supplies, and we have to get you guys some boots before the next snow hits."

He said, "You're coming, Henrico?"

"What do you think?" he asked. "Your mother's never driven a car with chains before!"

"Have you?" Fulton wanted to know, which was a good question.

Henrico didn't answer. He slammed the car into gear, and off we went along the icy roads 'til, two hours later, we pulled into a bleak, plowed Wal-Mart store parking lot.

I'd never heard of a Wal-Mart before and said, "Do—do they only sell walls or something?"

Henrico said, "If you don't like the name, stay in the car."

My mom told him, "He can't stay in the car, Henrico, I need to buy him some boots."

"With my money?" Henrico asked in a disgusted voice.

"With my money," she answered back, and climbed out. Leaning in, she wore an expression I'd thought was gone into the past. "Henrico, in Yorktown you were moody because you wanted to own your own restaurant. In Norfolk, you were agitated because the restaurant was failing. What is it now? On what basis are you such a tremendous prick now?"

He looked at her like how a dog looks when his nose is swiped by a cat's claw.

My mom slammed her door closed and started walking.

Me, Louise, and Fulton got out and slided after her. On our way, Fulton whispered, "I can't stand Henrico. If I had a credit card, I'd buy a gun and bury him."

"Yeah," Louise agreed.

I glanced at her.

Inside Wal-Mart, my mom said, "I know you all need new clothes, but we're limiting our purchase to boots. Understand?"

We nodded.

Louise asked, "Can we spend the money Dad sent us for Christmas?"

"Sure."

So me and Louise picked our boots. Mine were cheap rip-offs of L.L. Bean boots. Louise's were more like something a stuffed animal might wear. Done, we headed between Wal-Mart's gloomy shelves to the toy section.

In my pocket, I had twelve dollars, the last of my money from El Taste de Europa and some that my father had sent. Desperate to spend, I snagged the last two giant-sized *Star Wars* figures in the store. At a cash register, feeling stupid, I paid for Darth Vader and Chewbacca, even though I never liked him for playing.

When we got out to the car, Henrico was boiling mad over the things me, Fulton, and Louise had spent money on, even though they weren't any of his business. "You guys are such pigs. You waste money like no tomorrow, just like every other stupid American."

First off, I thought that if every other American did the same thing, why was he mad at us since we were American. Second off, they didn't feel like a waste, they felt hopeful, like buying them might change us into other, more happy kids. "What I got are cool," I said softly, holding up the huge plastic dolls I'd bought. Except I was beginning to wish I'd found something else or had saved my money since I only had a dollar left.

Fulton, who was reading, and Louise, who was playing with a toy hairdryer, ignored Henrico.

My mom said, "Leave them alone, Henrico."

Starting the car, he said, "I'm not allowed to say anything, but you make me spend money on their feet."

"It wasn't your money, remember?"

"Whose was it?"

"It's from child support," she answered. "I haven't spent a penny since we arrived."

He shook his head.

"Just be nice."

"I am."

My mom laughed harshly. "Come on, you're never nice."

Fulton looked up from his page.

Louise tensed.

My mom had never talked to Henrico that way, and I worried he might hit her. If he did, I knew I'd die. I'd roll over and quit on the unlucky world.

She went on. "In fact, you have dragged them from Yorktown to Norfolk to this hell hole. Your restaurant has left us in financial destitution, and you act like they're burdening you. Get it straight, Henrico, you're burdening them. You owe them."

Henrico's thick brows straightened to look like fat versions of Spock's straight ones. "I don't owe them a thing!"

"Really," she answered loudly. "Turn around and look at my kids. Turn around! They aren't the kids I had in Yorktown! Do you see that! Do you see what I see?"

He didn't look.

"Turn around," my mom demanded of him.

Gritting his teeth, including the dead one that was gray tinted, he hesitated before twisting and passing his bug-eyed gaze from Louise, to me, to Fulton.

"How do they look?" she demanded.

He shrugged.

"You know exactly."

He didn't speak for a moment, then he said, "Like crap. Like rednecks."

"That's right. Tell them sorry. Say you're sorry to them."

He refused. But at least he'd called us "crappy rednecks," meaning he'd noticed the truth of our unhappy existence by how we were becoming more and more disgusting. Unfortunately, the way Henrico knew the truth didn't make me feel better. It made me feel worse instead. I thought, *We have become crappy rednecks.*

In silence, we drove home, passing about seven pickup truck accidents and two flipped over eighteen-wheelers. The borrowed chains on our tires rumbled loudly beneath us like tank treads, and I imagined opening a window and hurling giant-sized Darth Vader and Chewbacca into a snowy signpost. All the while, my bothered brain felt like it was being a cannibal of itself, one part eating the other. I remembered back to the time when my father was being his grit personality and how he bent down and yanked the brain from the skull of a split pig that was cooking on a chicken wire rack. Slurping it back, he said in a real uneducated voice, "Them is good eatings." I wondered if the one part of my brain was telling the other part the same thing.

Tranquilizers

On the beach near our Florida home, before I take my deflated blimpness and go swimming, I'll sometimes stand up and search across the Gulf of Mexico. Usually in the afternoons there are storm clouds like whole cities hovering at the horizon. Closer to me, over the water's edge, I can see pelicans gliding in tippy formation, like they might lose control and crash on the beach in a pile of feathers and beaks and bird legs. Me, I see all of this and feel calmer after not being calm for years.

After our trip to Wal-Mart, I didn't think I'd ever feel calm again. We arrived at our employee-housing home after about two hours, and nobody spoke.

I got out of the car without Chewbacca or Darth Vader or my new snow boots and clomped down to my room behind the water heater and shut the door. On the floor beneath the big window, I read *The Hobbit*'s last few chapters again. I liked the end. It was a good book and made me wish I was Bilbo, except I didn't have his bravery or mental strongness.

When I finished, I sat still. I wanted to die, it was an overwhelming feeling.

Outside my window, snow started falling hard and thick. I hated seeing that. I was tired of snow and rolled to my lardy side.

A few hours passed and Fulton turned off the lights and television in the big basement room. I sat back up and wished that the plate glass window over my head would come out of its frame and shatter against my skull. Spinning on my butt, I kicked the wall beneath the window with my heels. Of course, nothing happened since that particular spot on the house felt thick as a piece of armor.

Standing, I turned off my light, opened my door, and stood beside the water heater. I unlocked the back door and went outside thinking I could maybe freeze to death.

The patio was buried in at least three feet of old and new snow that was still falling hard. I searched around. The undersides of gray clouds seemed to be pulling apart like insulation squirting out from between some rafters. I wished, I really, really wished, I hadn't wasted my money on Darth Vader and Chewbacca plastic dolls. I wished that because it made Henrico right about one thing. I wasted money. And if he was right about that, he was probably right about us being rednecks.

I continued looking up at the air. I didn't speak to God or anything, though. I'll be honest, I had begun to think God was a phony. To me, it seemed sort of lunatic to think an all-powerful bearded man would waste his life watching out for each person on earth. Plus, if he does watch people constantly, why does he let them get shot or killed in a car crash?

I lowered my head and noticed the old, rusty central-air conditioning unit sitting beneath my window. I went over and brushed the sharp corners off before feeling the edges with a thumb. Turning, I took two steps back, stopped. I heard a noise in the crummy woods behind me, making me hopeful that a mountain lion or wolf would pounce out and attack my jugular vein, but nothing happened.

I breathed out, still crying. The air conditioner clicked in the breeze, and I dove on it, striking a sharp corner so that pain shot through my fat-casing. Whimpering, I held my cow ribs as the area swelled.

I got up, stumbled back, and did it again, trying to knock the air-conditioner on its side. "Stop," I hissed at me. But I didn't. Shaking like an unbalanced washing machine, I staggered to my feet, took a breath, and dove at it once more, causing my right love-handle to gouge into the sharp point, hurting so bad that I by-mistake shouted as I toppled to the snow.

A moment later, Fulton came out from the back door. "What are you doing?" he asked.

On my stomach, I wondered myself as my lips started shivering separate from my control. I turned my face up and answered, "We got in a fight."

"What?"

"Me and the air conditioner."

"You're crazy, Cay."

"Fulton, I also hate myself like everyone else hates me."

He leaned over and saw what I was cupping. "Oh, shit! What did you do?"

"Nothing," I explained.

Snow twirled around his shoulders and stringy hair. I could smell his breath and wished I couldn't because it smelled like beef. "Damn it, Cay, are you trying to commit suicide or something?"

I shook my head. "It's just, I—I don't like me or Henrico."

He stared at me. "Cay, I can't believe you."

For a week, my injuries hurt so that I could barely bend or turn. The gouges looked like the claw marks of a dragon. For that reason and because they hurt so much, I liked all three, especially when they oozed clear water. When they finally scabbed over, I even picked them 'til they bled again.

I couldn't sleep or think. I kind of wondered if I'd tried to kill myself. My thoughts weren't normal. I got nervous that I'd seen a stranger hide behind the water heater downstairs, but my mom and Fulton looked around and couldn't find anyone.

Then two large bottles of triangular tranquilizer pills arrived in the mail. My mom had ordered them sent from our old family doctor in Yorktown, and I was supposed to take one brand before bedtime and the other in the mornings after breakfast.

"God, Mom," Fulton said, horrified, "they shoot bears with tranquilizers, and you're giving them to Cay? What's wrong with you?"

"This isn't the bear kind."

I held out a hand. I just wanted to get a pill in my mouth and forget.

"You're such a freak," he said.

"I am, yeah."

"This whole family is a joke!" he declared, and stomped downstairs to do nothing.

I swallowed a pill, but it didn't seem to tranquilize me except for how

I stopped worrying that the stranger lived in a secret passageway in the laundry room.

A couple of weeks after that, the Lake of the Ozarks's school system reopened.

It was like returning to a nightmare that I'd been scared awake from before. Nothing had changed. The halls and rooms were like midnight and smelled like Henrico's shoes. Once more, people mostly didn't like me. Worse, Kaiser constantly threatened me in the bathroom that I had to visit about fifteen times a day on account of injuring myself on the air conditioner.

For recess, we played in the gym, except I didn't. I sat on the stage and refused to participate in basketball games because I might've gotten embarrassed. I reread *The Hobbit* instead.

When it did get warm enough to go outside, the teachers located us on a narrow strip of brushed-off asphalt parking area in back of the school. I went and sat on a pipe with a meter on it. Two days in a row I sat there. On the third day, a kid with a disgustingly swollen black eye walked up and sat down, too. He smiled at me.

I lifted a hand to say hello.

"I noticed how you like *The Hobbit*," he said after a minute of staring at me from his pinkish, swollen eyeball.

"I like how the story goes." I closed my book.

"Except I wish there were more fights."

"Yeah."

He said, "Nobody reads around here. But me, I want to be a writer."

I nodded.

"I want to write stuff that everybody will read. I love adventure. If I wasn't going to be a writer, I'd be an explorer, for sure."

I looked down. I didn't want to do or be anything.

"You like science fiction too?"

I said, "I don't know."

"Do you ever draw pictures of scenes from *The Hobbit*?"

"I—I just read the book."

A wiffle ball struck me in my leg and a country bumpkin guy ran over and picked it up without saying sorry.

The kid sitting on the gas pipe said, "I keep a folder with pictures I've drawn. I want to draw every single exciting scene in the story. That's what I'm trying to do."

"Cool."

"You're Cay, right?"

"Yeah."

"I'm John."

I touched my fingertips to the gas pipe's flaky paint. "You don't come to school much, do you?"

"I got health issues." He leaned toward me. "Who's your favorite character in the book?"

"Bilbo and Gandolf," I informed him.

"Mine's Bilbo," he said to me, and pulled out a picture he'd drawn of how he imagined Bilbo to look.

Sadly, it didn't resemble the way Bilbo should've been. John's guy was fat as me and wore a clump of hair that didn't have any individual strands but seemed like an octopus laid on top of a round, Charlie Brown head. Also, his fingers, toes, and face had been erased and redrawn a few dozen times so that they appeared enclosed in gray, smeared fog.

"This is good," I lied, figuring I couldn't draw any better.

"I'm working more on details."

"They're hard."

"I can't get all his fingers on him without making it look like he's wearing baseball gloves."

"Yeah, it's hard."

At the end of our recess, he smiled widely at me so that his teeth showed like an old cemetery of crooked headstones that had been struck by lightning, kicked over, and partially eroded away. "See ya tomorrow, Cay."

"See ya," I told him.

◈

A few weeks passed. The sun grew warmer and the snow began to melt faster, forming lava flows of mud. The roads grew clearer and easier to drive. On account of that, people in three large pickup trucks arrived in Blackhead for a weekend vacation. They stayed at a summer home one down from ours and commenced to having a seventy-two hour beer-drinking, rifle-shooting party off their back deck.

They shot trees, stumps, cans, and even human shaped targets. My mom couldn't believe it and went out on our back patio and watched them blow off a few big branches of a pine tree. "This is it. This is it. I can't take this," she said, and went upstairs to her bedroom.

Louise chased after her and asked, "What, Mom? What?"

Climbing into bed, she said, "Nobody with any sense shoots in a residential area."

"But why does that make you go to sleep?"

"It's their stupidity. It's because of everyone's stupidity." She rolled over and turned her back to Louise. "Now please, dear, turn out my light."

Looking worried, Louise flicked the switch and came out into the hall where I was standing.

"Please, Louise, shut the door," Mom told her, sounding partially asleep already.

Louise pulled it closed. She peered at me and her eyes filled with tears. "Cay," she whispered, "what's—what's going on? Everyone doesn't seem right anymore but Fulton."

I gave her a hug even though I hated hugs.

We walked down the hall and into the kitchen but there was nothing to eat on the counter so we passed through it. "Is—is all this Henrico's fault?" she asked.

"Maybe. He is the biggest douche on earth."

"Yeah." We sat on the floor in the dining room. I had the feeling that I was floating and slightly separated from the solid world.

Louise said, "Why can't things be normal? You'd think God would make them normal after a while."

Being that she was young and more innocent than me, I didn't tell her how He probably doesn't exist. "Maybe Missouri is outside of his control . . . like Hell or something."

"Maybe," she agreed. A moment passed, and she smiled. "Except Missouri isn't hot, it's cold."

"Yeah." I paused to breathe and something loud and sharp struck the outside of the house.

Amazed, Louise said, "Cay, the house just got shot."

"No it didn't," I told her.

"What was it, then?"

I thought about it and realized she was right. Scared, I flopped to the floor and started crawling away like an army commando trying to save himself.

Louise followed. From the kitchen, I got up and rushed down the steps to the basement, where Fulton was watching a television show about fishing.

Louise told him, "We're getting shot at."

He glanced up. "No, we're not."

Struggling for air, I said, "A bullet hit the house. Someone must . . . hate us."

Fulton leaned back in his chair. "It's those grits. And they probably did it by mistake."

Me and Louise weren't sure, so we went into my room on our hands and knees and secretly looked out the plate glass window 'til we saw a few of the people staggering around drunk and aiming rifles at our roof like they wanted rain to come in on our heads.

Louise asked, "Does Lake of the Ozarks have police we can call?"

"I—I don't know, but if those guys want to kill us, they probably cut the phone line anyway."

We didn't die. The hicks were shooting at a raccoon on our roof. It was that way in Missouri, like you were living in a jungle, with partially toothless, unpredictable mountain men.

At school, I told John about getting shot at, and said, "You're lucky the raccoon didn't go down your chimney."

"Do they bite or something?"

"They'd take your finger off and eat it like a wiener."

"Like a wiener dick or a wiener hotdog?" I asked.

"Hotdog," he told me. "By the way, I'm writing a *Hobbit*-like book now, except mine's called *The Midget Lord*."

"*The Midget Lord*. Cool." The name mostly sounded unprofessional to me because, normally, people don't write about midgets and lords together. "Bet it's a lot of work."

"But it's fun work."

"I guess," I told him. But I didn't see how "work" and "fun" fit together very well.

John read me what he'd written so far and finished by explaining how Girt the Midget Lord crashes his horse through the gargoyle army cutting off heads and arms, before turning west toward where Murdock the Magician lives.

I was so impressed that I didn't know what to say. "That's really good," I mumbled.

"Yeah. It is. My mind just helps me write it. It just goes."

"I especially like the violence."

"Yeah."

I asked, "How does he get on his horse?"

"A rope ladder. It comes down from off the saddle when he calls for it."

I nodded, picturing the rope ladder uncurling magically so that Girt could get on board. I looked at John, "Do you ever wish you were a character in a story like this?"

He didn't hesitate. "Yeah. Do you?"

I lowered my head like a gargoyle. "No. I'm a wuss. I mean, I'm scared of *Star Trek* and it's on television."

He shuffled his pages and started sliding them back into a folder. "Like which episodes make you nervous?"

I explained, "I'm not scared of episodes, I don't like the show. I feel like it's . . . sort of trying to get me." I wondered if he might start laughing, which is what I probably would've done if I didn't understand what I meant.

"Well, they don't have televisions where the Midget Lord lives, so it doesn't matter. You could still be there."

Days passed. A weekend came and went. I started my own *Hobbit* version like John, except I called my book *The Leprechaun Barbarian*, because my main character, Heathcliff, was like a dwarf, except he was smaller and tougher and had better clothes. The beginning of my story went like this.

Have you ever herd of a Leprechaun? You probably think they only just go find gold at rainbows. But they don't just go to gold, they're famous for saving the world to. Before they spent there time doing gold, they were the toughest, most brave, handsomest, short people in the entire world, most especially a guy named Heathcliff, who grew up raised by wolves on Greenland because his mom and dad, who were really the king and queen Leprechauns, died in a shipreck. Thats sad. Its sad because Heathcliff would eventually have to clame his place as king and face the evil and magic Vulture Demon, who was evil and magic and trying to enslave all Leprechauns.

At school on Monday, I showed it to John.

"This is awesome," he said. "But—but give your Leprechaun a favorite weapon. Don't just let him use anything."

"Why?"

"Because, cool people have cool weapons."

Taking my story home that night, I reworked Heathcliff so that he carried a spiked axe. I brought it back the next day and John said, "Don't make the handle spiked, then Heathcliff can't hold his own axe unless his palms are extra hard."

"Well," I lied, "they are."

John scratched his chin. "Cool. I like extra hard hands. . . . Hey, look," he said and reached behind him and pulled a piece of paper out of his back pocket.

He gave it to me and I unfolded it quickly. On it was a drawing of a fat guy with pointy shoes and a feathered colonial-type cap. He had a scowl on his chubby face, a sword in his hand, and like two elbows on one arm.

John explained, "It's Heathcliff. I drew him for you."

"Wow, the hands're good."

"I sharpened my pencil so that I could do details."

"It's nice," I told him, feeling bad I hadn't drawn him a crappy picture of Girt the Midget Lord. Maybe it was what friends did.

That evening, I got out a piece of paper and worked on a sketch of Girt. After not-sleeping 'til 4:30 in the morning, I carried it to school the next day, except John wasn't there. In the cafeteria, a kid came up to me and said, "You're John's friend, right?"

I was worried he was going to pour something on me. "Ah . . . yeah."

"Well, I live in the trailer next to his, and last night, when an ambulance come, he told me to tell ya his daddy kicked him so he was carried to the hospital in Eldon."

His father kicked him! Missouri was like a bad movie where nothing but sad things happened to everyone and all lights were dim so that it felt like a permanent eclipse. I nodded and threw my drawing of Girt away since it looked more like a monkey in underwear.

That afternoon my English class went to the school library. I was by myself, hiding in the ancient shelving units and wishing I was in the *Hazel* television show, a show about a lady named Hazel who's a maid for the Baxter family. I was thinking of the episode where she drove a steam roller for some reason, and it was nice.

A girl named Cheryl came up and said, "Hey, Cay."

I looked up from imagining *Hazel*. "Hey . . . ah, Cheryl."

She had a nice face, a huge butt, and soft hips that were exploding the seams of her jeans so that it didn't seem possible they could stay sewed.

"Sorry about John. He was your best friend, wasn't he?"

I shrugged.

"His dad always beats him up, and he always comes back to school."

I felt stupid that I didn't realize why his face was usually injured.

"What book are ya looking for?"

I shrugged. I hadn't started looking since I was busy thinking.

"I'm searching for a romance novel. You know any romance novels?"

I shook my head. "No."

Cheryl smiled, and I saw that, for whatever reason, one of her front teeth was sideways, like a shark fin coming straight at you. "Caley, are we friends?"

I thought it was a gooberish question for her to ask since I hadn't ever actually spoken with her before. Still, I told her, "Yeah."

"Have you noticed I sometimes watch you through the skeleton in science?"

I shook my head.

"I do."

"Why?"

Cheryl grinned at me.

I didn't understand.

She leaned against a shelving unit that looked attacked by termites. "You think you might wanna go together ever?"

I tried to figure out her question. I glanced down at the holes at the tips of my sneakers that let the snow in when I walked. "Like, go out on dates?"

"No. We don't gotta do that."

I couldn't meet her eyes.

"You just gotta write me a note sometime."

"L—long ones?"

"Not if you don't want."

"I . . ."

"You wanna start going with me now? Or tomorrow, maybe?"

"Are—are you making a joke?"

"No," she said, sounding hurt.

"Now's fine."

"Good. I'll go write you a note in a few minutes, okay?"

"Okay."

Hours later, when me, Fulton, and Louise got back to the employee-housing house and were raiding the smelly cabinets for food, my mom came out from her bedroom and crossed her arms. In a voice like she'd been asleep, she said, "We're moving when school's through."

I looked up from the box of Twinkies I was reaching into.

Fulton said, "What?"

"Henrico accepted another job this morning."

I was speechless.

Fulton said, "I don't get you guys."

"I don't care," she told him.

"You think we'll go wherever you want."

"Yes, because you have to."

"Where's his new job now?"

"Florida."

"Florida," Fulton said softly. "Actually, Florida's pretty cool. I—I always wanted to surf anyway."

I wondered if our moving meant I had break up with Cheryl.

"Since we're going to Florida, can we skip going to Dad's this summer?" Fulton asked.

"Actually, we're dropping the three of you off there on our way. It'll give me and Henrico time to get organized."

Fulton bit at a Dolly Madison cake and chewed, leaving a smear of chocolate on his lips. "I'm not going to his house for more than a few days. I'm just not."

"Me neither," I mumbled.

"You're both going for about two weeks," she told us.

Louise said, "How about me?"

"All of you."

I went downstairs to my room and groggily fell to the dirty shag carpet. I opened my note from Cheryl. It said:

> You got good eyes and a lot of
> hair that's a nice color if you get
> near a lightbulb. I also like your
> accent.
>   Cheryl

I reread the note, and even though her ass and hips were huge, I liked the compliments and would've married her then and there if she'd asked. I'm glad she didn't.

The Bermuda Triangle

The next week, we phoned to tell my dad the news of us leaving for Florida, but he already knew from my mom. When it was my turn to talk, he got on the phone and I said, "Dad?"

He faked a sad choke, like he had a baseball of phlegm in his throat.

"Dad?"

"Son. Son . . . is that you?"

"Hey, Dad."

"You haven't written."

"I sent a letter the other day."

"Any pictures?"

"No, because you can't get them developed here."

"I believe you've forgotten about me?"

"No, I haven't." There was a pause, and it became obvious he wasn't going to talk.

I said, "I . . . ah . . . guess Fulton told you . . . everything and all."

"Told me what, Cay?"

"How we're gonna move."

"It's 'going to move,' son, and yes he did, and I can't say I'm happy about it."

I waited for a moment, confused, before asking, "Why?"

"Because, once again, your mother has sabotaged my plans."

"Plans for what?"

"Isn't it obvious, son? I have only recently been investigating the purchase of a second home in the Ozarks region, and your mother is now planning to relocate. I am forever a victim of her resentment."

"Okay." I scratched an itch on my face. "But you should be glad you didn't buy a house here. My—my only friend got kicked at a trailer park last night and was drove off to a hospital in an ambulance."

"We all hurt, son. Of late, my stomach's been killing me. It aches all of the time."

"Were you kicked?"

"I was not. Son?"

"Oh, well that's weird."

"Son, tell me. Why do you insist on using uneducated language and ridiculous colloquialisms?"

"What?" I asked, trying to figure out what he'd just criticized me about.

"You sound like a two-bit idiot."

"Oh, sorry. Here's Louise," I told him and handed her the phone.

Missouri was similar to the Bermuda Triangle, from what I heard, except on land. Everything always vanished and never returned, like furniture, my friend John, and my old self.

Without John at school, I had no one to hang out with, and because I was alone the Missouri mud-stompers swooped in like buzzards over a run-over deer on HH. In less than three days, I was back to being thought of as a snotty English kid with a crummy personality and a body like Winston Churchill, who during World War II was the president of England and said, "We will never surrender." He was also fat as a hippo and had a stuffy accent. We'd seen a film on him in history class, and a jerky kid pointed at me and yelled, "Winston!" But I wasn't like him. I wasn't British, and I had a lot more hair on my head. Winston was practically bald.

Later, while I sat in a corner of the study hall room, Cheryl came over for the first time since we'd started going together. She smiled and nervously sat across from me.

I said hello.

She wrote me a note and slid it over. It said, Write me a note.

Nervous to talk to her, I wrote. High.

She replied, Can you tell I'm whering my moms eye shadow and got one of her bras on.

I peeked up. I see the eye shadow.

She wrote back, I got to where the bras or I won't feel comfortable. I got large breasts now.

OK

She showed me the lacy red straps that went over her pale shoulders.

My crotch felt sort of weird.

I wrote, People say I'm like Winston Churchil, but I'm not. I got more hare, and I'm not British.

She wrote. This is a new shirt. Do you like it.

I didn't want to talk about shirts because there's nothing more boring. I answered, Its nice. Do I sound like Winston Churchill?

She told me, Last night my mom says I am a hore for going with you.

It was strange to be "going with" someone, especially someone who had such a big ass. I answered, You're not a horse.

She wrote back. Hore! My mom said hore! Can you believe it.

I answered, She can't spell.

Cheryl raised her eyebrows at me like I wasn't understanding something.

Because I thought she was mad at me, I wrote, If you're ever wondering, your butts not so big. I pushed the paper back and she gasped.

She scrawled out, You look like a disgusting fat blimp! And then she got up and moved to another table where her friends were.

After that, I was lonely. I wondered if maybe I shouldn't have written anything nice about her butt at all since she probably knew the truth about it.

Later in the day, me, Fulton, and Louise trudged to the lodge. Before going downstairs, I bought Cheryl a postcard with a picture of a sunset on the front. To me it looked romantic. I showed the cashier I hadn't stolen anything by emptying my pants and coat pockets on the counter, then I put the card in a pocket and went down to the deli, where I ate about twelve pounds of food including a pickle that was so big I had to wrap it in a napkin, and that's sick-looking if you've never seen it.

While I stuffed my face, Louise sat beside me and ate like a hundred malt balls.

Done, we went to the spa and looked at the ice cold pool water and decided we couldn't stand to go swimming and feel our chests tighten. So we looked at the whirlpool that was boiling, the yellow lights beneath giving the surface a volcanic, fiery feel. It didn't look good either.

I got on this belt machine that shakes people for exercise, except after a few minutes I could tell it wasn't doing anything for me. It was just shaking my blubber. I turned it off and considered riding the stationary bike, but I didn't because it didn't go anywhere. So me and Louise climbed on the weight machine and hung all over it like it was a jungle gym.

Instantly, Tony strutted over, shirt off and barefoot. He wiped his nose with a fat knuckle and adjusted his microscopic, red nut-hugger bathing suit. "If you don't use the machine properly," he told us, "you gotta get off!"

I watched at him from behind one of the machine's chrome bars. On the other side, Louise was testing her leg strength.

I started getting off.

He said, "Tell me, are you trying to get exercise?"

"I guess," I answered.

"You want exercise, I'll show you some." He cracked his knuckles. "I'll show you how to get strong. You like that? You want to be strong?"

"Okay," Louise told him.

"Not you, your brother."

I shook my head and said, "Ah, no thanks."

"It's good for you," Tony snipped, his massive man-boobs like two brown hubcaps on his chest.

"I don't like to learn anything anymore."

"You're gonna like this." He went and fetched two boxing gloves that were on a hook near a punching bag that hung from the ceiling. While I sat on the bench-press bench, he came over and tied the gloves onto my clammy hands.

Tony put on a pair, stepped forward and punched the punching bag so that it leaped and swayed back and forth. "You wanna try?" he asked.

"No."

"Try," he ordered me.

Because I was a coward who couldn't tell him to go put on a shirt and pants, I got up, and hit the bag, which barely moved. "It's heavy."

"It won't fall. It's held by a chain"

I told Louise. "Louise, it's like hitting a wrecking ball."

She came over and touched it. "Why do people hit them if they're not soft?"

Ignoring her question, Tony let loose with a series of jabs and swings that caused the bag to jump and shutter. Stopping, he hopped on his toes like a boxer and scooted all around. Done, he told me, "Practice on the bag for a minute, then I'll show you boxing."

"No thanks."

"Eh, you see the *Rocky* movie with Stallone?"

I nodded distantly.

"It was uplifting, right?"

"Yeah." I punched the bag some as he walked through the empty spa to check the chemicals in the pool.

Louise told me, "This is boring."

"It hurts my wrists," I told her. "The gloves don't help."

She said, "Watch," and ran forward and bumped the bag with her shoulder. Smiling, she spun around and told me, "I think . . . I broke . . . my arm."

Tony came back.

"You ready for your lesson?" He put his hands up to protect his weird, chunky face with his gloves. "Go like this," he said.

I did.

He said, "Now punch me." He took some shots at both sides of my head, the air snapping so that I knew if he connected with my face it would collapse like an exploded soccer ball. "Now you do that to me."

I did what he showed me, only my hands didn't make a snapping sound.

"Harder! Harder!" Tony demanded, bouncing forward and striking me in both shoulders. "Now punch back. You must punch back!"

I tried.

"Can we go?" Louise asked.

"Quiet," Tony told her sharply, and hit me in my chest, sending a jolt down my spine that felt like hot nails in my heels. He grinned.

I lowered my hands.

He said, "You can't quit." He stuck his face out at me so that I could sock him. "I'll give you free swing."

I swung limply at one of his tanned cheeks.

He ducked me and drove a fist into my mouth so that the hinge part of my jaw felt like it stretched back to my ears. I felt my whole head snap back before I held my gloved hands to my lips to keep from bleeding all over the floor.

Louise said, "Cay. Cay . . . you got blood coming out of your nose, too."

Tony stripped off his gloves. He had a look of satisfaction on his face, like he'd finally gotten back at us for all the times we'd annoyed him about temperatures. "You let your guard down," he told me, yanking off my gloves.

I went back to the men's dressing room and ruined three brand clean Lodge by the Lake towels with my blood. Feeling sad and unlikable, I got out the postcard I'd bought for Cheryl and stared at it. I flipped it over to the blank backside. Mouth-blood dripped onto the place a stamp should have gone. Annoyed, I wiped the card off and put it away.

At home, my mom made frozen chicken patties while Fulton and Louise watched *Star Trek* and I sat scared in my room covering my ears and speaking loud so that I wouldn't hear a single noise from the show. At dinner, my mom took a few bites and caught sight of me. She put her fork down. "Cay, what happened to your face?"

Fulton said, "Tony beat him up."

"Tony? In the spa?"

Louise said, "Yeah, Spa Tony."

"Cay, do you mind explaining?"

Louise told her, "Tony was teaching him boxing and gave him a free hit at his face, but it wasn't really free because he ducked and hit Cay in the mouth," she said, acting the scene out. "It cut his lips so that when he ate cake, it turned red in his mouth."

My mom said, "Jesus Christ, Tony hit you?"

"To show me boxing."

"He's a grown man, a weight lifter. He has no business boxing you, Cay."

I put my fork down. "'Cause I don't look strong enough to fight?"

"No. Because he's an adult." She stood up. "Come over here."

I got up and went over. She lifted my chin and looked at the backside of my swollen lips. Her neck flushed red like sunburn. "What the hell is wrong with this place? It's incredible. God, you're lucky you didn't lose your front teeth, Cay. Really." My mom took a long drink of wine. "What in the hell is wrong with this whole damn place? Can anyone tell me?"

Louise raised her hand like she was at school. "I think what's wrong is we're out in the middle of nowhere without very much furniture."

Cheerleader Boots

Who would guess that in the spring tiny flowers sprout up through dead Missouri weed patches? Thousands of them come through the earth but none have color, or much color, which makes them not as good as regular, bright flowers. They reminded me of flimsy Polaroid pictures from an instant camera where you peel back the plastic piece of paper to show the yellowish picture that's always too yellow.

At night, I thought about those flowers. The way they were almost colorless made me feel low. I missed real color. I also missed sleeping like a normal person. Even with my elephant tranquilizing tranquilizers, I hardly fell to sleep easily. Sometimes I stayed up rolling and wishing that I was somebody living in a state with color who wasn't so unlikable and could sleep.

At school for a week, I entertained myself by starting a book called *Lord Foul's Bane* that Fulton had bought. It was scary mostly on account of the main character having a disease called leprosy, which is something that gives you rotting flesh. I read the description a few times and, by chapter three, was sure I had it on a knuckle. I smelled the area for a stink, but it was okay. No matter, I had to quit with the story. Catching leprosy got me too nervous to read.

About that time, during recess, Kaiser came up and said, "Hey."

I stayed quiet.

"What, ya ain't speaking, Winston? Well, tell me . . . do ya like this?" he asked, slapping my head.

I didn't answer.

"You like this then?" one of his friends said, and did the same thing on my skull.

"How 'bout this?" Kaiser demanded, slapping my cheek.

I told them, "I have leprosy and now you've got it. Soon your skin will rot off like mine, and I'll laugh at you for how gross you'll be."

Kaiser pinched my earlobe hard and walked away.

I thought how I hated them but was scared to fight back for fear they'd beat me 'til I'd end up like John with his ruptured spleen. If my dad was around and in his army mood, he would've been sickened by me and placed me on a diet and commenced a huge muscle building exercise routine for me. If he was in his businessman mood, he'd have waved a hand at me like I wasn't worth thinking about. And if he was being a college professor type, he'd probably just watch like it was strange how sad and stupid I was.

But I was leaving. It didn't matter. I constantly reminded myself of that.

Then, one morning John said, "Hey, Cay."

In the dark hallway, where I could hardly see my hands, I turned, nearly smiling. "You're back."

Even though his face was sunken in from losing excessive weight, he smiled.

I asked, "Did—did you watch a lot of television?"

He nodded. "It was boring."

"What's it feel like if you don't have a spleen?"

"I can't tell that it's gone."

I adjusted books under my arm. "Why—why'd your dad do it?"

"Because me and Mom don't show him enough respect for the way he drinks beer all day and night."

"Oh."

"Hey, Cay, guess what. I got twenty more pages written in my book. You gotta hear them. It's almost done."

I said, "Are you gonna sell it?"

"Yeah. Then me and Mom'll move. See ya at lunch." He left for his first class in weeks.

I started down the hall toward my own class when a girl named Wendy, one of Cheryl's friends, stopped me. "Cay," she said, her hair similar to a strange sea plant that can reach for fish. "Cheryl told me ta tell ya you're not going together no more."

I said, "Why? I—I didn't do anything."

"No, ya didn't do nothing at all, 'cept give her a card with a bloody thumb print and write one letter."

I wanted to say I was shy, but I actually didn't want to win Cheryl back. I'd come to realize that Cheryl's ass and hips were too huge. The other thing I'd noticed about her was that the first finger after her pinky was shriveled so that her fingernail wrapped around the top of it like a little helmet. That caused me to wonder if she might truly have rotting flesh.

Wendy hissed at me, "I hope ya know ya done broke her heart! She'll never be the same."

I tried to explain myself. "The—the card wasn't meant to have blood on it."

Wendy widened her stance to show how much she hated me. That's how I noticed she was wearing high, white cheerleader boots with her jeans tucked in the top. Her body shape was square, but she was kind of sexy for wearing such cool boots. "I—I like your boots," I said, thinking they made her look like a tall, mature woman.

Wendy placed a hand on a hip that wasn't much smaller than Cheryl's. "I'm one'a Cheryls best friends, Cay. You can't say them things to me."

"Sorry."

"Ya better be, swine," she snapped, and marched into the darkness. As she disappeared, I couldn't help thinking that if Cheryl had worn cheerleader boots I might've liked her more.

I turned and went into my class. Sitting there, I suddenly got so damn lonely for Cheryl that my jaw got tight and creaky like a bad door. The thing is, when her clothes hadn't smelled musty, she'd smelled pretty good. How could I have let her go?

When I saw John at lunch, I was feeling desperate to have Cheryl back. Sitting down, I tried not to talk about my problems by asking, "Does your spleen hurt when you eat?"

He chewed a French fry. "No."

"That's good." I wanted to talk about Cheryl but said, "I'm still working on *The Leprechaun Barbarian*."

"That's a great story."

"Not really."

"I'm being honest," he said. "Hey, you wanna hear mine?"

"Sure." But I really didn't.

"It's forty-three pages, so I'll just read you the last five so you know the end!"

When he finished, he asked, "How was it?"

"Professional," I told him, but I wondered if the *Midget Lord* would be better if Girt, the hero, didn't always battle and just thought sometimes about being a midget and a lord.

"You think Girt's cool?"

"Yeah. He's tough."

"Good. A midget's gotta be."

With John back at school, Kaiser left me alone again. I didn't know why. He was either scared of John or scared of catching leprosy. In study hall, John and me drew pictures of dwarfs, elves, and hobbits stabbing or blasting arrows into monsters while Cheryl and her friends watched me hatefully. Except when Wendy wore her cheerleader boots, I didn't care at all.

"Look at them," I told John.

"Stupid," he agreed. He was a good friend that way.

I said, "You wanna spend the night this weekend?"

"Really?"

"Yeah."

He accepted without even checking with his parents, and that caused me to get nervous he didn't have a bedtime schedule to maintain exactly, like me. Also, I got scared that my mom was going to be upset at me for not asking for permission, which she was.

"Sorry," I told her quietly.

"Cay, you know I don't like to drive around here."

"Yeah."

"Then why'd you say I'd pick him up?"

"'Cause his mom works on Saturday and his Dad isn't allowed to drive."

She took a deep breath. "God!"

"Sorry, Mom. I am."

She held a hand off the table. "Don't talk to me right now? Don't say a word."

"I won't," I promised.

Leaving to fetch John on Saturday afternoon, she seemed better.

Fulton stayed home reading a book, so it was just me, my mom, and Louise driving up twisty HH, over the steep hills, along the razory cliff edges, and into the town of Osage Beach, with its pathetic, gap-toothed, rundown streetway of still-closed seasonal T-shirt dealerships and trinket stores that sold fake Indian things like tomahawks with rubber blades and piggy banks shaped like canoes. We passed the driveway to Lake of the Ozarks Elementary and Upper, located behind an old house and a hedge of dead bushes. We drifted down the long roadway to the Bagnell Dam, which looks flimsy and sounds like a type of bag. We crossed it and at the far side turned and shot off into the muddy countryside where big clodhopper Ozark families like Kaiser's sit around cooking liquor in their tubs and skinning rodents to check the sharpness of their knife and for fun.

For ten minutes, we roared past brown fields and wooded patches of toppled over trees or stumps 'til we saw the sign for the Pen Oak Trailer Park, except someone had scratched out the P and the K and scratched in an F and T, making it Pen Oak Trailer Fart. Pulling in, we putted down the lumpy dirt path and came to a round lane that was bodered on both sides by dozens and dozens of weathered and crooked mobile homes that didn't seem like they should be legal for people to live inside.

Louise said, "They're all gross."

"They aren't," I informed her, but they were.

We drove along the circle past a trailer that had burned down so that its base and charred wooden frame were all that remained.

We stopped at trailer number 17. As I got out to knock, the trailer's narrow front door flew open, clapping against the tin siding. Waving happily, John leaped down the cinderblock stairs, a bunch of notebooks tucked under an arm. He grinned at me and slipped into the car.

My mom said, "Hello, John."

He fidgeted and said, "Hello, ma'am. Thank you for picking me up."

"My pleasure. John, do you have a coat? You might need one."

"I won't. I have a naturally too-hot body."

"Any bags? You are spending the night."

"No, ma'am, I sleep in my underwear and use the same clothes over."

"Good. That's good," she said, shifting into gear. I closed the door and we went around the dumpy circle and back out to the main road, where we started back toward Blackhead.

Passing over the Bagnell Dam, John said, "One day I wanna put really big, floating tires on a pickup truck and drive it in the water. Do you, Cay?"

Before I could answer, Louise asked, "Why?"

"'Cause, I've been thinking about it."

We were off the dam, and John said, "Look at that, place. It's called Whacky Wally's. I love it. He's got the best T-shirts. I wish you'd live here 'til he opens in June."

My mother said, "John, I hear you want to be a writer."

"Yes, ma'am."

"Are you a good student?"

"No, but I miss a lot of school on account of my dad's 'unprovoked anger.'"

My mom asked, "Unprovoked anger?"

"It's what the lady from the state called it when she visited me in the hospital."

I hadn't exactly told Mom about John's spleen.

She asked, "What happened to put you in the hospital?"

"My dad kicked me 'til my spleen had to come out."

"Yuck," Louise said.

"That's awful," my mom agreed distantly, but she didn't say another word 'til it was almost dinner time. Then all she said was, "I decided not to cook, so go eat at the lodge, okay?"

John, me, Fulton, and Louise left down the crummy street and passed through the woods and to the bottom of the hill. We skirted the trailer park, which smelled of old fish, and went straight to the Deli, where I got two sandwiches and the last slice of carrot cake.

John got two sandwiches, chips, and candy.

Fulton picked a piece of pizza and tried to convince the woman behind the counter to give him a beer. She wouldn't.

Louise got one sandwich, a Firewater soda, and her feet-smelling candy.

As we ate, John said to me, "Cay, why're you breathing hard?"

I raised my shoulders like I didn't know.

Louise said to him, "My mom thinks he's sick."

"I'm not sick," I said, angrily, checking John's expression to make sure he didn't think I had something that might cause him to breathe hard, too.

Louise ate some more foot candy. "She thinks he can't handle stress."

Fulton said, "Shut up, Louise."

I stood up. "Mom doesn't think that!"

"Uh-huh."

"She doesn't. I've asked. And that's not why I'm breathing hard."

Louise said, "If you're so normal, what about *Star Trek*?"

Horrified, I glanced toward John, but John wasn't paying attention. He was looking around the wide room at the bowling alley, the juke box machine, and the spa where Tony had recently mashed my mouth.

"This is nice. It's real nice."

"Yeah," I told him.

"You know what? If I had your house and all of this stuff around, I'd never be bored."

I explained, "It gets boring. It just does."

"Not for me."

"After a time, it would."

Louise said, "Have you ever bowled every day? Have you ever met Tony?"

"No."

"Well, neither is so good."

Following dinner, we went to the theater, which was playing *Wizards*, a cartoon about wizards. I hoped it would be like a movie version of *The Hobbit*, but it wasn't. It took place after a nuclear holocaust that turned people into dwarfs and fairies and elves, causing me to start to sweat down my back and at the edge of my hairline. I don't like nuclear holocaust movies since they're about everyone dying.

When *Wizards* was done, John, me, Fulton, and Louise walked home in the darkness. The whole way, too, I felt like we were being watched by creatures from the movie so that I would have run if John wasn't there.

Passing into our house, me and John got snacks and carried them to the basement, where I went into the bathroom and, to calm down, got my nighttime tranquilizer. Coming back out, I found John showing Fulton his story and drawings of the *Midget Lord*. "The whole thing's practically one big fight," John was saying.

"Radical," Fulton mumbled, really looking like he enjoyed what he was seeing.

John told Fulton, "You should read Cay's book. His is great, too."

Fulton glanced up. "Didn't tell me you were writing a book, Cay."

"I forgot."

"It's called the *Leprechaun Barbarian*," John told him.

Fulton balked at the title. "That's the worst name I've ever heard. It sounds like a joke."

I grit my teeth. "I—I gotta go to bed, John. Just come in to sleep when you want, okay?"

He appeared surprised but answered, "I'll probably watch *Saturday Night Live* with Fulton."

"Sure," I whispered and went off to lay awake on the floor since I was giving him the cot. Later, John came in and began snoring. A short while after that, I got so terrified over a nuclear holocaust that I got up and ran to the second floor, where I went into Louise's room, crawled beneath her bed, and rested there awake like a dog who's scared of thunder.

In the morning, as soon as I did fall to sleep, Louise stepped on my head causing her to scream in terror.

My mom came in and found me rubbing my temple.

"I stepped on his head," Louise told her. "But I didn't know he was there."

I crawled out from beneath the bed. "It's okay. I don't mind."

She tightened her bathrobe belt. "How'd you get in here?"

Not wanting to feel embarrassed over myself again, I thought before answering. "I . . . must've slept walked. I sort of remember doing it. It's all like a dream."

She raised her hands in surrender.

In the afternoon, after lunch at the lodge, John, me, Fulton, and Louise walked back to our employee-housing house and got into the car so that my mom could take John home.

While Fulton, who was in front, tried to convince my mom to let him drink a beer when they got home, Louise told John about a story she might write with two bears, a mouse, a duck, and a doll baby that's alive.

"Where's the action?" he asked, sounding like a book writing instructor. "Ya gotta have action, huh, Cay?"

"Yeah," I agreed. "It's usually better if you do."

John said, "Maybe give one of the bears a ray gun or the mouse a jet pack."

I looked at Louise and couldn't help thinking that John was right. Both things would make the story better.

"But how about the dolly?"

"Give her a crossbow that shoots poison arrows?"

She frowned at him. "I can't give her something like that. She's nice and likes to wear crowns and jewelry. She's going to marry one of the bears because she likes his Christmas store and how he wears a red vest."

John said, "Look, don't let anyone get married, it ruins a story. Think of something else. Think. . . . Hey, wait a minute. You said there was a duck? Make the duck evil. Wouldn't that be awesome?"

"No, because the duck's nice. He lays golden eggs."

John rubbed his cheeks. "Listen, Louise, there're good parts to your story, but I don't think it'll work your way." He held up a hand. "But you should try. Writers always have to try. And my word isn't the final word. Understand?"

"Yeah. The thing is, I like nice stories."

John seemed to have suspected that. "It's sad, Louise, but nice stories aren't in style anymore. They're too nice."

Blinded by the Light

At the start of the last week of school, I went to the bathroom and Kaiser pushed me against a dark stall and gave me a Missouri Tornado, which is, I sorely figured out, when an asshole like him grabs your boy nipple and turns it like a knob on a television 'til you start screaming on account of it hurting so much. My nipple was so bright pink looking that two days later, when I was tossing the ball with Louise on the pool deck, Tony, with all his overlarge muscles and skimpy red bikini bathing suit, frowned at my sore boob. "Missouri Tornado?" he stated.

I didn't answer since he'd slugged me in the mouth a few weeks before.

"Hey, tell me. How come I have to say to you a hundred times, stop throwing the ball on the deck?"

Louise held it. "Sorry."

"It's not professional spa behavior."

I looked around the big room and down at the icy pool water that the rule was me or Louise had to dive into if we dropped the ball. Annoyed at him, I sputtered, "But—but it's empty. No one's in here."

"You always complain," he told me. "No wonder someone gave you a Missouri Tornado."

When we got home that night, Henrico was in the kitchen wrapping dishes with paper and setting them in a box for moving. "Eh," he said to us like it was a threat, "you pack your own Goddamn rooms. Your mother and I won't do it for you."

"Fine," Fulton told him.

We went downstairs where Fulton went to the television but didn't turn it on even though it was nearly five and time for Spock and Kirk to "explore new worlds." He picked up some of his paperback books and put them in a box. "Cay?"

"Yeah?"

"Why does *Star Trek* scare you when it's so fakey?"

I shifted my eyes to his borrowed Lodge by the Lake cot and its unmade sheets that were brown from not getting washed. I couldn't find a reason for my fear or even how to explain it. I shrugged.

Fulton dug his hands in his pockets. "Cay, you need to stop being crazy now. Okay?"

I could feel my face get frying-pan hot with embarrassment.

"Cay, after we leave here, tell yourself you're getting normal again."

But I wasn't sure I could. "I want to . . . Fulton."

"Good. That's good." He nodded and started toward the television, except the wind from his movement caused a piece of wall paneling to unfasten and fall against his head, slapping him like giant ruler. Annoyed by the surprise attack, he pushed the wide sheet of wood to the gross carpet. "Can you believe it?" he asked, annoyed.

I whispered to him, "The wall did that on purpose."

I can imagine what a whale thinks if it gets shot by a harpoon. In whale language, it probably goes, *Oh, God, it feels like a shark bit me.* After that it probably thinks, *If I live, I'll never be careless again. Everything will be different.*

Like a whale, I was thinking the same thing. I thought that something in me had been hurt, and I would never be so careless again. I'd never go back to Missouri, and I'd never live in a place with six blizzards while I was trapped without furniture and stuck with a drainpipe that rats climb from. I'd never go bowling anymore or swim in a too-hot hot tub or eat so much free food I'd get overweight. I'd change everything. As soon as I was free, I would do everything different except not-meet John. To me, John was amazing, sort of a miracle, the way he stayed bouncy and cheerful despite his trailer home and his violent dad who drank too much beer.

That's why, on the last day of school, while I thought about the things I'd change, I carried a present up to the bus stop and stood about ten feet from

Stacy, who was wearing a plaid skirt decorated with a giant safety pin with a raccoon tail or something dangling from it. Like a zombie, I was staring at her pencil legs, thinking that the hair growing on the area behind her knees was really cute. Her face was, too, excluding how when she looked at me or Fulton she made a sneer on it, like somebody had hypnotized her to sneer whenever she saw us. I wondered what she'd think if she knew I was carrying, wrapped in newspaper, a giant, plastic Chewbacca doll.

Fulton said, "I can't believe you're taking that retarded thing to school."

I ignored him.

"He looks like an ape."

Louise told Fulton, "He's cute."

"Cute like a gorilla with hemorrhoids."

Louise said, "What're hemorrhoids?"

"Painful bumps on your ass."

"Do people really get those?"

"Yeah," Fulton said.

"You think I will?"

"Probably, yeah."

I told them, "I—I always wished Chewbacca could talk. In the movie I wished he talked. I—I also wish he wore pants. People need pants."

"He's not a person," Fulton told me sarcastically.

"I already know he's a wookiee," I shot back.

I noticed Stacy watching me, her lip snarled up. I figured she thought I was the ugliest kid she'd ever seen, so to get away from her and Fulton, I walked to the edge of the road to wait for the school bus.

Louise followed me and whispered, "Cay, guess what? I know what you mean about pants. He seems naked."

"Yeah," I told her.

We got to school and halfway through the day, a kid in the hallway acted like I was a pig by calling, "Sewwwwy! Hey, sewwwwy! Sewwwwy!"

I hoped he was calling to someone else when he said, "Hey, Winston! Ya hear me, don't ya?"

I kept going.

At lunch, John and I sat away from everyone else so that I could give him his present.

"Wow," he said. "I didn't bring you anything."

"It's okay." I ate something that was supposed to be a taco.

John tore the paper off Chewbacca and studied his plastic purse and gun that looked like a crossbow. He smiled. "I love this. I love Chewbacca, man."

"Good."

"He's so strong."

"Yeah, he takes his arm and knocks people over. I—I saw you looking at him when you spent the night."

John put Chewbacca on the table, adjusting his feet so that he stood like a miniaturized wookiee. "Where'd you get him again?" he asked.

"In Eldon. At the Wal-Mart."

"He's so real looking."

"He's molded nice." I sat forward, suddenly scared that John, who was so friendly, was going to be killed by his own drunken dad. "Hey . . . don't let your dad get you anymore. Okay?"

He laughed. "He won't stop." He picked up Chewbacca, cradling the big thing like a newborn baby. Staring into the figure's eyes, he said, "You know, Cay, I wish you weren't going away. Do you?"

I studied his jumbled, dark and light teeth and lied, "Yeah." I didn't want him to think I wanted to leave his friendship.

"Ya think Florida will be more fun?"

"Maybe."

He ate a few more boiled French fries. "Ya know, I won't have any friends after ya go."

I knew he was right, but I said, "Anyone'd be your friend," which wasn't true at all. John was different.

"I'm gonna keep Chewbacca forever."

I couldn't smile, but I wanted to. I even felt like giving him more than just Chewbacca for being good to me. If I'd been a good person, I'd have included giant Darth Vader, who I didn't like anyway.

When we stood, John surprised me by giving me a hug, which made me uncomfortable and worried he was queer.

"Bye," I said to him.

He wiped at his eyes and grinned. "Bye, Cay. Don't get sunburned."

A few hours later, me, Fulton, and Louise were on the bus rumbling down HH. I fisted and unfisted my hands, watching the knuckles turn white. For some reason, I was actually sad to be leaving, which was like being sad about getting your leg released from one of those spring bear traps with steel teeth. It made no sense.

"Blinded by the Light" played loud and the lake, now almost completely unfrozen, glistened in a sort of yellow light that looked cast from a church's stained glass window. It was pretty enough, almost like a normal lake. I stared out at the shoreline of trees and rocks and suddenly wanted to cry. It was so stupid. I hated that place, but I wanted to go home and take all of my tranquilizers and rest flat on the filthy wall-to-wall carpet and cry for what I was losing. I'd miss John and Cheryl. I'd miss a few things, meaning Missouri couldn't have been as crappy as it actually was.

So Happy to See Us

The next morning the movers came. In the rain, it took them about an hour to put the few things we owned in their truck. When they were done, Henrico drove us out of Blackhead for the last time. He turned onto HH and struck a big pothole that unfastened the muffler or something so that it started vibrating like someone was trying to do highway repairs beneath our feet. It vibrated the whole rest of our trip.

In town, we headed across the dam. On the far side, we went northeast in the direction of St. Louis. We didn't stop once for three hours. We rumbled across the muddy, bleary, tree-stump-decorated state with the muffler jackhammering constantly below our butts so that if Henrico had let us play the radio, we wouldn't have heard it anyway.

Hours later, we looped around St. Louis and roared over a flat bridge across the Mississippi River, arriving in the state of Kentucky. We were out of Missouri.

Fulton put his head out the window and yelled, "And we aren't coming back!"

Louise said, "Yeah," and shook her little fist.

I didn't do anything. I waited to have something happen to me so that I wouldn't be fat and unlikable and crazy anymore. I waited, but it didn't occur. I put a hand flat against the window. "Please," I begged under my breath.

Nothing.

Feeling robbed, I scanned the Kentucky grass and roadway and decided that it did appear slightly more green and hopeful than Missouri's bleakness. Kentucky was a better place to be. Then again, I figured anywhere was a better place to be until ten minutes later when we screeched to a halt and were caught in the worst traffic jam of our whole lives.

"Goddamn it!" Henrico shouted, shaking the steering wheel.

My mom said, "Cool down."

I saw Henrico's lion face in the rearview mirror and wondered if he'd been planning to drive all of the way to Yorktown that night. After an hour, he was stalking up and down the roadway beside the car.

Other people were doing the same thing. It was hot out, too. Blurry currents of heat rose off everyone's hood.

In our car, we sat. We adjusted. We sat on different parts of our butts. Then I had to pee. At first, I tried to ignore it since I knew my needing to piss would cause a scene. Whenever we traveled, if any of us had to pee other then Henrico, he thought we were trying to ruin his day and night and maybe whole year.

I clamped down harder 'til my bladder began feeling like it was filled with needles sticking me. Nearly crippled, I looked outside for a nearby place to hide behind, but it was barren like the moon. The whole place was a giant work site, and all of the trees had been bulldozed and dragged away for a new road or town.

Sweating, I said, "Mom, I gotta pee so bad."

She nodded. "Go."

"How about Henrico?"

"He'll have to deal with it." She waved me on with a hand.

I stepped out of the car and Henrico spun around and shouted after me, "I leave you here! I leave you here, punk!"

About a hundred yards away, I got behind a giant cement drainpipe that was turned to the road so that everyone was able to see me if they wanted. As I started peeing, the traffic jam that hadn't moved even a centimeter actually started creeping forward. I hurried, scared I'd be abandoned at the border of Kentucky and Missouri. Done, I zipped up and scrambled from around the pipe as fast as I could. Running like an uncoordinated business guy in a disaster movie, I arrived back to the car just as traffic stopped.

Fulton craned his neck out the window. "God, Cay, you peed on your pants."

I looked down and he was right. There were splatter streaks going down my legs. "I was rushing."

"Gross," Louise commented.

"It's just a few spots," our mom told us. "It'll dry."

But Fulton and Louise acted as if I smelled like a zoo for the whole rest of the day 'til we arrived at a small motel in Burnt Prairie, Kentucky, with its views of corn fields and a McDonald's that glowed similar to an alien space ship in the *Close Encounters* movie. Along with our shabby luggage, we snuck Punchy into our room in a boat bag. So that she wouldn't destroy anything, we locked her in the bathroom before going to the McDonald's.

At McDonald's, me, Fulton, and Louise sat in a separate booth from my mom and Henrico, who weren't talking to each other because I'd asked for two Big Macs and Henrico said, "Two! You need two Big Macs like a hole in your brains."

I didn't say anything, but my mom snapped back, "What do you care, Henrico? If he wants two, get him two. You're getting reimbursed."

The thing is, after that I didn't want to eat even one Big Mac.

I asked Fulton, "You want my extra Big Mac?"

He grabbed it.

Then I wanted it again.

We returned to the motel, and Henrico and my mom disappeared into their room and we went to ours. Fulton and Louise flopped onto the beds, while I went to let Punchy free. Opening the door, I discovered she was surrounded by strange white fluff, like stringy snow, that hadn't been there when we'd left her.

"Look," I said.

Louise came over. "What is it?"

I stepped forward. "It's like long pieces of yarn."

"Where'd it come from?"

I went and picked some of it up. "Don't know."

Fulton tromped in and rolled the stuff between his fingers. "It's the bath mat. Punchy ate the bath mat."

Punchy wagged her tail.

"Man, Punchy," I said, wishing she hadn't done it. "What if Henrico finds out?"

"He might kill her," Louise whispered.

Fulton rubbed Punchy's smoothish otter head. "We'll carry the shredded stuff out to a garbage can. He won't know."

But even if he didn't, I was feeling so let down that Kentucky hadn't changed me, Henrico, and our luck that I doubled up on my tranquilizer and rested on the bed feeling pinned down like a bug to a bug collection kit.

We arrived in Yorktown about six in the evening. We entered the small downtown and rumbled past a green battlefield that had clouds tilting over it like soap suds sliding off glass. We passed above the York River so that you could see the distant cliffs where my father liked to blow off his guns. Four or five minutes later, we turned into my dad's neighborhood, where in the past I'd spent a lot of time wanting to escape.

Arriving at my dad's, we sat in the driveway for a moment before Fulton got out. He wandered up past two new cars and knocked on the front door as if he didn't care whether it was answered or not. After a minute, he came out. He was followed by Kora, who was so happy to see us that she put a hand over her mouth and played like someone was pushing a feather down her throat. Then she went back inside.

I got from my seat and closed the door behind me hoping my dad might do like on TV and rush over and give me a hug.

Dressed in boxer shorts, a stained T-shirt, and some really ugly leather sandals that looked like two unraveled cigars with a squishy rubber sole sewed on, my dad froze, his eyes riveted on me. He cleared his throat as if he was too touched to talk, and said, "You're fat."

On the other side of the car, Louise said, "I'm here too, Dad." She didn't know that calling me fat wasn't a compliment or even a little affectionate.

He nodded at her and said to me, "You're totally out of shape."

"I ate too much in Missouri."

"Eugene!" my mother spoke firmly, climbing out of the car. "Have you arranged for their flights?"

"Yeah!" He glared.

"Well, what're the dates?" She put her hands on her hips.

"They're flying down on the sixteenth of June."

While they spoke, Henrico got out of the car, silently picked our bags from the trunk, and placed them on the gravel. Done, he got back in the car.

My mom turned and hugged Fulton, Louise, and me. She said, "Bye," slipped back onto the passenger seat, and Henrico drove her away, the tailpipe chattering like a machine gun. I wondered if they were escaping away from us forever, except who could stand to be alone with Henrico for the rest of their life?

None of us spoke.

My dad, wearing his underwear-boxer shorts, turned around and started walking.

Fulton said, "Should we follow you?"

"What do you think, son?" he answered.

Inside the house, my dad closed the door. He breathed deeply and exhaled, like he was trying to tolerate us except that it was hard. "Kids, let me tell you how I feel. I'll be honest, too. I am unbelievably embarrassed by you. You look like hell. Do you know that? You look like a bunch of country grab asses."

Fulton and Louise didn't answer, so I mumbled, "We know." But it's funny to have someone in their underwear say you look like a "grab ass," whatever that is.

"Cay, has anyone other then me told you you're obese?"

"Yeah."

"Do you realize that your appearance reflects on me?"

"No."

"Well, it does."

Fulton rolled his eyes. "Come on, Dad, he knows he's big."

He examined Fulton intensely.

Louise said, "I got all A's on my report card."

"'Course you did. Think of where you were. You were in the middle of goddamn nowhere, with a bunch of redneck-jackasses who could hardly hold a pencil much less write a two syllable word."

Louise didn't say, "Thanks."

Mangled!

The next morning, my dad shook me awake before sunrise. His breath smelled of stale beer and stomach stink from burping, but he was dressed in real shorts, the same shirt as the day before, and running shoes. "Get up, soldier."

I sat up, groggy from having stayed awake most of the night.

"Dress in clothes you can run in."

I started putting on my jeans.

"No! No! Shorts," he snorted.

I slid into the shorts I'd peed on and my other shirt, and we went upstairs and out the front door, where I ran with him for a few miles, nearly killing me. When we got back, I sat down sweating in the grass while the ground wobbled to the beat of my pulse.

"You're going on a diet," he said, pointing down at me. "Twice a day, you'll run to the river and back. On top of that, I'm severely limiting your calorie intake."

"Okay," I said quietly, worried I was going to puke.

We went in for breakfast, and he gave me a dill pickle. It was my dad's idea of food that would get me less chunky.

"But, I sometimes like to eat more," I told him.

"That's in the past."

"But . . . I can't only eat pickles, Dad. I'm supposed to have bread before I take my tranquilizers."

He stepped backwards like I'd just told him he had cancer. He rubbed his chin and flattened his lips in disgust. "Whoa. Tranquilizers! Did you say tranquilizers?" he asked in a booming voice, so that my stepbrother Barney, who was in the other room getting ready for his last week of school, could hear. "You're on tranquilizers?"

I nodded. "Is that bad?"

"Buster, they're drugs."

"Maybe, but I started taking them for not sleeping and always feeling like I was holding onto an electric wire."

He bit his lower lip. "Well it's time you faced the real world. Where are they?"

I hesitated, scared to live without them.

"Where, son?"

"My bag, downstairs."

He pushed me aside and stomped downstairs to the guest room, where Fulton was still asleep. He got my bag and found my bottles of pills and dumped them into the bathroom toilet.

I looked down at them and considered lapping at the commode water they were dissolving in 'til my dad flushed it, causing the pills to circle and disappear. Feeling panicked that I might feel panicked, I could hardly hear him lecturing me about how I was behaving like a drug junkie, which is a person hooked to drugs, which made me guilty feeling that I was a junkie. Over and over in my head, I thought, *How did I become a junkie?* for two or three hours straight.

For three days after that, too, I considered myself a junkie, and I hated me for that. Also I felt antsy, like my skin was loose on the muscles and bones of my body, causing me to tremble and sweat, which I especially did when we had to go with my dad to his work, something I hated. Similar to when we were younger, we were assigned to sit quietly in his storage room where he stacks the things he buys to save money on his taxes.

In his storage room, he had three shotguns and two rifles, army ammo boxes, and a series from Time Life Books called *The Old West*. He had televisions that weren't getting used, two stereos, and a CB radio. He had stacks of plates and dishes, a chainsaw, and a handgun that was the same brand owned by James Bond. He had a Weed Whacker, big knives, and nice new snow boots alongside flashlights that were nearly the length of baseball bats. He had a fancy kerosene heater, rolled up rugs, and a few footballs, which I didn't pass with him anymore since he only throws them like he's trying to kill you.

"So, what're we supposed to do in here?" Louise asked.

"Just sit," Fulton told her.

We were quiet and bored for a few minutes, then Fulton said, "You know what sucks? He buys all this crap for himself, but he never buys a few chairs for us to sit on."

I kneeled and selected *The Gunfighters* from the *Old West* series.

Louise said, "Is this the way we're going to spend our whole trip?"

Fulton opened a pocket knife he'd found in a box. "Not me," he told us, closing the blade, and slipping it into his pocket. He got up. "I'm going to see Dad about us leaving." He went out the storage room and shut the door behind him.

I stared at Louise. "It's weird that we don't have anything, and Dad's got stuff he doesn't need."

She shrugged. "I don't want this stuff."

"How about just a pistol so that Henrico would stop being mean?"

Before she could answer, Fulton came back with permission for us to leave.

"Where're we going?"

"Anywhere we want. All he said was not to bother Kora at the house."

"That's it?"

"And to be back by five."

We passed by the secretary, out the door, and down the front walk.

We went along a grassy hill, turned, and wended our way into town, which isn't really a town as much as some places to eat and a beach store. We stopped and stood in front of the Cannon Ball Restaurant, which is a pretty funny name for a place for eating. We crossed over the road and stood in the sand of the public beach.

Yawning, Fulton kicked off his shoes and walked up to the water's edge, where he stuck his toes in. Louise followed.

I didn't get any closer. I was worried it might make me feel sad since the last time I'd dipped my toes in salty water was in Norfolk, where I'd felt sad for being a thief and a beer drinker. I turned and walked along the grass strip between the street and sand. It had thousands of disgusting cigarette butts and soda tabs in it.

Turning, I looked up the big river, past the massive steel bridge that is scary to drive on. Feeling guilty for being a junkie, I watched cars go back and forth wondering why they didn't skid and fly off. If they did, I could save the passengers by swimming out to rescue them. I needed to do something good to make all of my bad wash partly away.

Shortly, somebody tapped me on my shoulder.

I turned.

Louise stood smiling.

"What?" I asked.

"This!" she said, and threw sand in my eyes.

Spitting, I shouted, "God, Louise, you . . . bastard!"

"What?" she wanted to know, standing back.

"You can make someone blind with sand," I explained, stumbling down to the water and flushing my eyeballs out.

Fulton came over and said, "What happened?"

"Stupid Louise threw sand in my eyes!"

Louise said to Fulton, "Why'd you tell me to do it?"

I paused from washing my eyeballs. "You told her to?"

"He said I should."

"I told her to do it because I was trying to give you something to do other than think, Cay."

Somehow it made sense. "Oh," I said, before realizing I was in the salty water that had made me nervous, but it wasn't making me feel sad. Instead, I was less sad, so I decided it wasn't the same water as Norfolk water and that I should swim in it more, not less, in order to feel normal.

◈

A few days later, my dad got home from work and glugged some beers. When he had a six pack inside his gut, he took us to go hunting in the woods above the river. I was given a shotgun and Fulton a deer rifle. My dad wore his camouflage army clothes and a big, floppy cowboy hat that matched. About his waist, on an army belt, he had a smallish pistol, two big knives, and ammo packs. The rifle he carried had a scope screwed to the top. I don't know who he was being, but whoever it was carried a lot of weapons and a know-it-all attitude.

After parking, off we went, through the woods silently. Time passed, and my dad said, "There's nothing in the world like this, is there, kids?"

Louise asked. "What're we trying to catch?"

He chuckled. "Anything. Hedgehogs, squirrels, muskrats, raccoons, possums, and maybe even a crow or seagull. Anything we see."

Louise stopped. "Are we gonna eat them?"

"You ever heard of anyone eating seagull, crow, or hedgehog? It's trash meat."

She was quiet for a moment before saying, "Dad?"

"What?"

"Last year a teacher told me people should only hunt for food and . . ."

He snarled, "That's a typical Missouri liberal's position, Louise. That's who was teaching that class. A Missouri liberal."

Fulton said, "Maybe we should shoot cans? We used to do that some. Remember?"

"Christ!" My dad said, digging a heel into the dirt.

I told him, "You know what, in Missouri someone hunted a raccoon on our roof. They even shot at it while we were in our house. But, guess what, I don't think they got it, though, because I didn't see it lying up there later with blood all around. You know? And—and I was sort of glad they didn't get it." I told him softly, "That's just how I felt."

Dad stopped short and threw his hands in the air like a crazy cowboy trapper. "Is this what you guys have become, pacifists?

Fulton said, "No."

Louise asked, "What's a pacifist?"

Dad huffed out beer-smelling air. "Look it up in a dictionary. It's the only way you'll learn it."

Fulton lowered his gun. "It's just, I don't feel like shooting something for no reason, Dad. I think that might be normal."

"Normal for pinkos and commies, Fulton. Killing small animals isn't a crime, boy. It says so in The Bible."

The three of us didn't know The Bible very well, so we didn't know if there really was a chapter about people having the right to shoot seagulls for fun.

"But . . .," I started.

He pointed at me. "Mind your place, fat boy."

His words struck me like a cannon ball from the Yorktown battlefield. I was so shocked, I stumbled backwards even, nearly falling to the ground and digging the barrel of his shotgun into the dirt. Even though I was on his pickle-and-Tab-soda diet, my dad still thought I was a pig. He still thought I was just a gross kid that embarrassed him if ever people saw us together.

"What? You don't like getting criticized, Cay?"

I couldn't talk.

"Your feelings are hurt, huh? Well think about mine."

Fulton said, "Dad, maybe don't call him fat anymore. Maybe that's all it is."

My dad's face flushed red like his raw elbows. He glowered hard at Fulton, shouldered his rifle, and started walking back toward his car.

Confused, Louise said, "Are we quitting already?"

Over his shoulder, he told her, "You're damn right we are. I'm not going to let you guys question my judgment. I'm the father. You're not the father, I'm the father. I'm the adult. Okay?"

"Okay."

"So don't act like shooting things is wrong if I tell you it's right."

Louise was trying to catch up with him. "I didn't mean to."

He ignored her all of the way back to where we'd parked. Then, driving home, he kept having spurts of anger that caused him to pound the dashboard with a fist, as if a fly kept landing on it.

The next morning, though, he wasn't mad at all. He'd completely forgotten about us questioning his Bible knowledge. I stood out on the back porch of his house, my stomach rumbling like a bowling alley. My dad must've seen me, because he came out, too. Squatting, he nuzzled his nose against my ear like I imagined girls might do but not a father.

"Caley?"

"Yeah."

"The entire time you were away, my heart ached."

I stayed silent because mostly I wanted to get my ear away from his nose.

"I'm so proud of you," he said, and sloshed his tongue across my lobe.

I thought about my dad's weirdness over the next few days. Me, Fulton, and Louise hung out on the public beach beside the Yorktown commercial district. We talked about my dad and Kora. We said that Barney Boy was gay and that Hugh was smart to always be gone from the house. Then, one afternoon, Fulton spotted a kid he'd gone to junior high with.

Fulton went over. They started talking. They laughed and left to smoke cigarettes and get bloodshot eyes from, I think, taking pot.

It happened the next day, too, so that I told Fulton, "You shouldn't do that stuff, Fulton. You'll get addicted."

"Stick it, Cay."

"But I know what it's like to have a drug problem. It's terrible."

"What is?" Louise wanted to know.

"Nothing," we said, not wanting to corrupt her too much.

I was concerned that my dad might discover how Fulton was taking marijuana. I couldn't help it. Also, I'd noticed that whenever Fulton did, he ate dinner using his fingertips instead of a fork and his eyeballs looked painted pink.

Usually, after supper, when my dad and Kora weren't nearby, Barney made a point of calling me "Fat Albert." He'd walk by and say, "Hey, Fat Albert." By calling me Fat Albert, he was meaning that I reminded him of the Fat Albert cartoon character who wears a ratty red sweater and plays music in a junkyard band.

Early in our visit, Fulton had defended us against Barney Boy. But when Fulton started leaving at night to visit his middle school friend who was doing dope and guzzling beer, me and Louise were stuck alone with Barney, who was like a person trained to torture people. With Fulton gone, he even announced that the big downstairs television was his television and he was the one who got to decide what channels to watch.

"Hey, Fat Albert, you like *Laverne and Shirley*?"

"Yeah."

"Too bad. When it's over, I'll find something you can't stand."

"Okay," I said. But he wasn't so hard to trick. Me and Louise told him we hated the shows that we liked so that, thinking he was torturing us, he'd turn them on.

No matter, there was a lot of tension in the television room. It made me and Louise wish Barney would drop dead. We even talked about accidents that might suddenly kill him, leaving us to pick our television shows.

"How about poison?" she asked once.

"Poison isn't an accident. Maybe a poisonous snake," I told her, thinking I could find one somewhere.

Halfway through the second week, Barney didn't come home one night. Excited, I told Louise, "I just had a vision." I put my fingers to my temple. "He's been mangled!"

"Are you sure?"

"Almost."

We jumped up and down and turned on the television show *CHIPs*. Relaxed, we watched Ponch, one of the stars, eat a Ho Ho snack cake while he sat on his motorcycle.

Then, upstairs, we heard the door crack open and slam shut. A few minutes later, Barney came down. He glanced at the TV and shook his head. "We ain't watching this." He turned it to the *Donny and Marie* show, which is a repulsive variety show about Donny and Marie Osmond, who are a sister and brother who sing a song called "A Little Bit Country and

a Little Bit Rock and Roll." He's rock and roll, and she's country, but what they really are is terrible. Plus, they have teeth so bright they must have been eating mayonnaise sandwiches their whole lives.

I said, "Please, let's don't watch this, Barney. *CHIPs* is better, don't you think?"

"What's wrong, Fat Albert, you got a crush on Eric Estrada?" He was meaning the actor who plays Ponch on *CHIPs*.

"No. It's just Donny makes me feel sick."

"So what do you want instead, Fat Albert?"

"Another program. Anything."

"You probably don't mean anything. You probably don't mean *Star Trek* since it makes you wet your pants."

I froze.

He smiled.

My knees started to shake. "Who . . . told you that?"

"Your dad. He thinks you're pathetic."

"I didn't tell him."

"Fulton did, Fat Albert."

"Stop calling me Fat Albert, Barney."

Behind Barney, Donny was singing some song that was grating on my nerves.

I got up and started back to the room I shared with Fulton.

Louise called, "Where are you going, Cay?"

"He's running away," Barney told her. "He can dish it out, but he can't take it."

I stopped. I'd walked away from so many Missouri rednecks, but walking away from Barney seemed unacceptable.

He said, "Your whole families alike. You think you're important but you're just dicks. You ruin everyone else's lives because you're so screwed up."

I replied, "We don't ruin other lives."

"You don't? You're so fat if you sat on someone you'd kill them."

Louise chimed, "He's less fat, now."

Barney walked over toward me.

I told him, "We're not dicks."

"You mean you don't have one." He pushed me. "Gonna cry, Fat Albert? You gonna burst into tears?"

My bottom lip shook feebly. He shoved me again so that I stepped backwards. In my whole life, the only person beside Fulton I've ever gotten in a punch fight with was Barney. I hated him.

"What do you weigh, two hundred pounds?"

Louise said, "He's not that much. That's like a car."

"Yeah, you're right, he's more like a truck."

Furious, I charged Barney the way a bull charges a matador, with my head out in front.

Instantaneously, Barney caught me in a headlock and all I could do was struggle helplessly. My temples began to feel like a big empty nut that might crack. "Fat Albert," he said. "Fat, Fat, Fat, Fat, Fat Albert."

Louise yelled, "Stop, Barney!"

He tightened his grip.

Desperate, I struggled to get free. I tried to punch him but couldn't. I pulled to loosen his arms. Finally, I reached down and scratched one of his bare legs all of the way from his kneecap to the top of his thigh, drawing blood like I'd used the sharp prongs of a garden tool.

"God!" Barney hollered, throwing me to the ground. "You fight like a girl."

I didn't reply.

He leaned over and blew cool air on the vicious-looking injury. "God," he groaned, hopping on one foot like his scratched leg wouldn't hold him. Eyes watering, he said, "These might need disinfecting."

"They're just scratches," I called, as he went upstairs.

Kora treated me like I'd used a switchblade on poor, defenseless Barney Boy. She treated me, Fulton, and Louise like three out-of-control hooligan thugs with crappy manners and barbarian personalities. She hated us with a bigger hate than the original hate she'd had when we'd arrived in town, and she'd nearly thrown up just spotting us then. It was scary.

The Life (or What)

Our final Saturday in Yorktown, my dad woke up being like Charlton Heston. He kept his jaw jutting out and spoke in a movie script way from Charlton's famous Bible movies from Egypt.

We were sitting at the dining room table. It was lunchtime, and there was tension so that the air felt fragile, like invisible glass lacing.

He finished his hotdog and stretched his arms. In a booming voice, he said, "A fine enough repast, Kora."

Kora, who wouldn't look at us, growled, "Eugene, shut up."

"Yes, fine."

"Better yet, Mr. Annoying, come here."

They got up.

Fulton dropped his napkin onto his plate and went downstairs. Me and Louise carried dishes into the kitchen because that was our punishment for injuring Barney.

Behind us, Barney limped past, pretending his damaged leg had hobbled him.

Hugh was at work.

Upstairs, we heard Kora boom, "That had better be tha last meal I eat with them punks'a yours, Eugene."

"Oh, Kora, punks they may be, but they're also family who have wandered far astray of the herd, who have become the proverbial black sheep."

"Listen up, Eugene! I am a Christian woman. I am a forgiving woman. But they ain't my family, Jose. I don't raise that sort of rubbish."

"Kora, please. I . . ."

"Good lord, just shut up, Eugene! Shut your disgusting mouth. It's simple. I want them outta here. I can't stand 'em looking cross the table at me!"

"But, where can we go? Kora? Do you . . ."

She cut him off. "Ya make me wanna barf, Eugene! Go anywhere. Anywhere."

He came downstairs. He stood defiant, like a superhero with his feet apart and his chest out. "Leave the rest of the dishes and pack a few things to spend the night out. Tell your brother."

In the basement, I told Fulton, "We're leaving for somewhere in a few minutes."

"For where?"

"I don't know."

He grabbed his extra shirt, and the three of us went up and out the front door to his car.

A couple minutes passed, and he came out. We got into his car, and he drove us out of the neighborhood, down the battlefield roads, and out to Route 17, where we glided into a 7-11 convenience store parking lot to buy beer.

Sitting behind the wheel, my dad guzzled five cans without stopping. That's when his throat suddenly cracked and he blurted in his Charlton-Heston way, "I give and give and nobody ever gives back. I treat you kids and Kora, dear Kora, with loyalty and love, and you despoil my good intentions. Am—am I doomed to live this way? Is there no one out there to treat me as I should be treated?"

We didn't speak.

He looked at Louise, who sat nervously beside him. "Am I doomed?" he questioned her even though she was only eight. "Am I doomed to be injured by those whom I care for and love?" He started up the car and we hurtled down Route 17. He gulped at another can of beer and dropped the empty on the seat. "And—and I bet I know what your mother says about me. She's turned my children against me. Isn't that so? She fills your head with lies."

Fulton sat forward. "She hardly talks about you, Dad."

He got another beer. After a minute, he said, "That so?"

"Yes."

"Dear Lord, lend me your ear and tell me what I did to deserve this?" He took a long swig and stopped. He burped loudly. "Worst thing is this is happening to me. That's the devilish aspect of it all." Ten minutes later, he merged onto the interstate. Forty minutes after that, we drove past Norfolk, hooked east, and rocketed along 'til the interstate abruptly ended in the city of Virginia Beach.

My dad steered us along through the city and turned onto Atlantic Avenue. We drifted lanes briefly before he suddenly pulled into a hotel parking lot, causing me to think we had reservations, which was sort of a good surprise.

My dad got out of his car, went over and sat on a stack of patio furniture that had just been unloaded off a delivery truck. "Looky here, kids, they arranged a throne for me to regain my energies while you swim in the ocean." He blinked from behind the yellow lenses of his Foster Grant sunglasses.

Louise said, "You're staying here?"

"Resting up, child. How do I look?"

Louise told him, "You're good," because what else could she say.

Me, Fulton, and Louise walked around the hotel, over the boardwalk, and down to the busy beach.

Louise said, "Fulton, is Dad too drunk to drive?"

I stopped. "Of course not."

Fulton punched my shoulder hard. "He can hardly stay in his lane, Cay."

I hadn't noticed since I'd been staring at my thinner face reflection in the window.

We swam and returned to where my dad was supposed to be.

He was missing, and we wondered if he'd been arrested for sitting in the new chairs illegally. We leaned against his car and waited and waited 'til he came stumbling from the hotel bar.

"Are ya ready ta go, young ones?" he asked, flopping into his Oldsmobile and starting the engine. Shifting into reverse, he hit the gas and ran over a chaise longue, malforming it pretty badly. "Shit," he mumbled and gunned it onto Atlantic Avenue, where he cruised around before locating the highway and starting for Yorktown.

Fulton sat forward. "Dad?"

"Yeah."

"Ah . . . should you be driving?"

"Me?" We drifted sideways, and a car honked beside us.

"Yeah, you're kind of all over the road."

In the front seat, Louise looked partway petrified.

He slammed a fist against the steering wheel. "Did I truly ruin that chair or something?"

"I think."

He snickered and swerved some more.

Louise begged, "Please stop, Dad. Please."

"Ya want I should bring an end to our journey?"

"Yeah."

"I'll take that into consideration." Shortly, we crossed over the Hampton Roads Bridge Tunnel, and he veered off the interstate, around a big off-ramp, and into the parking lot of the Strawberry Banks Motel, which was located on the shore of the Chesapeake Bay.

Wordlessly, my dad went into the motel office. Ten minutes later, he came back to fetch us. "Got us a beautiful room." We followed him down the lineup of doors 'til he stopped and opened one. He entered first, dropped his duffle bag, kicked off his sandals, and commenced to stripping off his shirt and pants prior to collapsing on a bed. Even before the bed springs stopped squeaking, he was drooling on a pillow.

Fulton swiped the room key from out of the door lock, and the three of us went outside and sat beside the seawall. The bay washed loudly against rocks, and we looked out at all the anchored freighters resting in the Hampton Roads, which is a weird name since it's not a road but water.

We'd sat for about an hour when Louise said, "You think he's drunk now, Cay?"

"Yeah."

Fulton picked a bent cigarette from out of his pocket and lit it.

Time passed, and it grew dark so that only the lights on the big ships remained visible. Fulton spoke with his head down. "Sometimes I think I might like to join a ship and sail away."

"Yeah," I agreed. "But . . . I'd miss Mom."

Louise said, "If they're metal, how do they float?"

"I don't know," I told her.

Then we heard Dad's knees clicking and turned to see him approaching in nothing but his boxer shorts. He got to us and said, "Come on," and started walking along.

Fulton stood. "You're naked, Dad."

"Got my bathing trunk on, boy."

"They're boxer shorts."

"Fulton, if you want to abolish our pleasures, we would prefer you depart. Right, Cay?"

I didn't want to agree.

"Cay, tell him."

I hated myself but mumbled something that wasn't English and didn't mean anything.

Fulton turned and left.

Me and Louise, like two lost puppies, followed behind my dad. He went along the wall for about fifty yards before he veered to the right, crossed some burnt grass, stumbled on a bottle, and arrived at the slate patio where diners were eating seafood and watching him. Without a second thought, he staggered between their tables and up through the sliding glass door to the dining room.

Wishing we were invisible, me and Louise followed behind past the bar and all of the tables. I felt like a baby walrus following a big walrus with bumpy skin problems.

He stopped at the front entrance to the restaurant and held onto the stewardess's little podium. "Got anything for a fine feast?"

I was sure she'd say no because if I worked in a restaurant I'd understand that people sitting around tables paying for food wouldn't want to be so close to somebody without a shirt and a nearly-exposed penis that might flop out of the slit in his underwear fabric at any second.

"Like what, sir?" the lady asked my dad.

"Fish," he told her.

She gave him a menu and he ordered.

When we arrived back at the room, we were carrying three aluminum foil packages of dinner that I couldn't have because none of it was a dill pickle or a diet drink.

I gave the one in my hand to Fulton and sat down on a corner of the bed unsure what to do. I stared at the wall and listened to everyone eat until I suddenly felt so let down that my empty stomach seemed painfully full.

When my dad was done, he wiped his mouth, rolled from the bed, and turned on the television, switching the channels 'til he found a fake wrestling match. He crawled back on the bed and rested on his back. After a couple minutes of watching the news, he rolled over. "Louise," he said, "come give me a backrub."

"Dad . . ."

"Louise, I'm your father," he said sharply.

She reluctantly shuffled over, hesitated, then got to rubbing his acne scarred shoulders that feel like lumpy, melted cheese.

"Ooooh, that's nice," he told her. "Hold, ah, that's good."

Louise didn't talk.

"So, kids, what do you think? Is this the life or what?" Dad asked in his Bibleish, Charlton Heston voice just before he groaned in pleasure from his back message.

He was right. It was the life. My life. And I wished it wasn't.

Parts of the Same Being

The morning before we left Yorktown, I ran to the river and back. Thankfully, Kora was off to get her hair done when I returned. More thankfully, she hadn't said goodbye to me.

Hugh, who we'd hardly seen, came up and stood around. "Sorry it's always so weird," he told Fulton.

"Yeah."

"Our parents bring out the worst in each other."

"Seems," Fulton agreed.

My dad, meanwhile, was being his nostalgic and holy self, which I hate worse than any other of his persons. On the road to Richmond International Airport, he looked bloated and uncomfortable, his hair wet and shaped like a raccoon that had been struck by a car so that all four legs were in the air. "We've come to this place together and now we leave apart," he announced sullenly.

The summer sun turned the dry grass orange and white, like tiger stripes. I looked up at the trees and they seemed greener than before, so colorful they looked fake. I rubbed my eyes because it seemed like my eyeball lenses had something on them, but nothing got less colorful.

"We must live with the knowledge and peace that time and God's binding love will see us together again."

Fulton rolled his eyes.

We pulled off the highway and drove down a few roads before arriving at the airport. Inside, we picked up our tickets and headed for the airport lounge, where we sat in black plastic chairs and looked out at the hot runway. My dad put his hand around Louise and said, "I'm dying inside."

Louise seemed to be getting crushed under his muscles.

"And so I lose my children once more. Once more they depart my life and the joy that they brought me will vanish to gray."

Momentarily, a speaker crackled on, and our plane started boarding passengers. Me and Louise gave him a hug. We took our empty bags and started down the ramp to the plane, but before I disappeared from sight, I stopped and looked back. I loved my dad, which, like I said earlier, I was embarrassed to admit because it's hard for me to admit it about anyone, especially him. It sounds girlish too. But I do love him, and I wanted to say something nice since I was sad to leave no matter how sore he made my stomach feel from worrying or how many selves he had become during our trip.

"Bye, Dad," I said.

He waved back. "Watch you don't get fat again, son!"

Nodding, I caught up with Fulton and Louise and off we flew to Miami, where we transferred to a small propeller plane that reminded me of a black and white movie about someone going to China. That carried us over to Naples.

In Naples, the captain and copilot parked the plane in a painted circle and the stewardess in her high healed shoes flipped the door outward on a hinge, so that it turned into a pair of steps to the ground.

Me, Fulton, and Louise dragged our bags out the door and across the runway through the hottest heat I'd ever felt before arriving at the airport entrance door where my mom and Henrico waited.

Smiling, she gave us hugs and kisses on our cheeks, while Henrico, being Henrico and basically hating our guts, looked at us like we were lepers, which scare me, with misformed faces and dropping-off fingers.

We stood around talking for a few minutes before my mom said to me, "How did this happen?" She waved a hand up and down so that I figured she was meaning my getting normal weight.

"At dad's. I didn't eat anything but pickles and diet drinks."

She seemed taken aback. "Pickles and diet drinks?"

"It's true," Fulton said darkly.

"That's insane."

"Least I'm not gross-looking," I told her.

My mom shook her head. "You were never gross-looking. It was in your head."

"I don't think. I was embarrassing to Dad."

"Please, you didn't embarrass anyone, and you can bet," she stated harshly, "that I won't allow any diets like that around here." Then the happiness at seeing us seemed to vanish, and we trudged to our un-air-conditioned car and drove and sweated to the Sandy Gulf Motel, where we were staying until we could find a house.

Pulling into the parking lot, Henrico directed the car toward a long, low cement building that had six sets of doors with small windows. We stopped and parked by one set. Me, Fulton, and Louise got out and pulled our bags from the trunk.

Inside the place reminded me of a basement. It was dark. It smelled like mildew. Plus, there was Punchy all nervous and shivering in a steel dog cage.

"God, why's she there?"

"She ate one of my good shoes," my mom explained.

I went and patted her.

Henrico shoved past us on his way to the bathroom, went in, and shut the door.

Louise said, "Hey look, Cay, they got a miniature stove and kitchen sink in this room."

"It's an efficiency," my mom told her, putting her hands on the back of Louise's shoulders. "We can make meals in here."

She said, "You think it's kind of dirty, Mom?"

"A few stains. That's all."

That night, in the room that me, Fulton, and Louise had across the courtyard from my mom's and Henrico's, as the non-see-through plastic curtains shifted in the breeze from the air conditioner unit and big crawling bugs made noises in the bathroom trashcan, the sinking part of my brain kept me awake once again. Scared that I had been followed by my problems and bothered from missing Dad, I went outside to the courtyard and sat by the pool holding *The Hobbit* so that I might read it and feel better. But I didn't read. I felt too bad 'til I fell asleep. Then, at sunrise, I was awakened by planes roaring overhead and shooting smoke behind them that I found out later was mosquito spray. Getting up, I watched the planes fly back and forth over Naples 'til they were tiny on the horizon.

All of us ate breakfast in my mom and Henrico's room, including me. She made me eat a piece of toast with butter, which I don't like any more due to all of the calories, and some eggs. Then Henrico left for work. With him gone, the four of us walked up the street to a beach that was broad and white like ground pearls. Its edges were trimmed by a pale wall that was covered in bright lizards. Seeing it, I was glad to be there. I hadn't been glad that way in years.

After swimming, we walked back to the Sandy Gulf, and my mom smiled and closed her door to watch a talk show while me, Fulton, and Louise went out to explore. We walked downtown, which was only a few blocks away, then we circled around and around the shopping district, stopping in a magazine shop to look at paperbacks and get a secret glimpse at the cover of *Playboy* magazine, which Louise said was disgusting but still stopped and looked at, too.

Later, when we were passing by a 7-11, Fulton pulled out a wadded twenty dollar bill from a pocket and offered to buy us Slurpees.

"Where'd you get that?" I asked.

Fulton grinned. "From Kora."

"You mean . . . you stole it?"

"That's what it sounds like."

Louise looked into the convenience store window. She turned and said, "I want a Coke Slurpee, all right, Fulton? And I'll put the straw in. Don't do it for me."

"Cay?" Fulton asked, snapping the twenty dollar bill in my face.

"Just get me a Tab diet drink, please."

"A Tab. A crummy Tab? You can go off your goddamn diet now."

I shrugged. "I'm off it."

"Whatever," said Fulton, and when he was inside, I leaned against the window and watched him, worried he was going to steal something. He didn't, since he had already stolen Kora's twenty, thank goodness.

Mind Like Paper

The huge afternoon thundershowers and the low-flying mosquito-spraying planes that buzz Naples in the early morning, like the rustle of palm trees and the burpy bark of alligators after dark, became familiar to me even before we left the Sandy Gulf in August.

When we did leave, we moved to this house, with its backyard on a golf course that looks good for playing football on. Inside, there is the automatic garage door that you press a button to run and that causes Henrico, when he's home, to scream if anyone does it a few times in a row. But I don't care so much anymore about his screaming since he explodes the same way if I try not to make him mad or if I don't. He's like disarming a stick of dynamite where you always cut the wrong wire.

Since leaving Missouri, my madness and weird discomfort have faded. But it's not gone. Maybe they'll never go. Maybe they'll always stay as long as I remember them. It was an unhappiness that swallowed me like quicksand, then unnaturally stained the backside of my skin an unattractive color. At least, that's how it felt.

But I try not to sink from it anymore. I'm doing everything differently, like I said I would. When I have free time, I walk down to the beach or over to this outdoor racquetball complex by the mall where I hit a tennis ball with my mom's old tennis racquet that came from Oklahoma in another box they'd found of our stuff. It's nice and free and nobody bothers you about sounding British or snobby or playing racquetball with a tennis racquet.

When I'm done hitting, I visit a bookstore across the parking lot inside the Coastland Mall. That's where I eyeball fantasy novels with good covers. That's where I'll probably see *The Midget Lord* soon alongside the *Chronicles of Corum* and *The Dragon Riders of Pern*. That's also where I tell the ladies I'm not stealing and they tell me they know. I don't show them my underwear to prove it, but they don't ask to look, either.

Louise has made friends. She plays with the neighbors' granddaughter, Emily, who is always visiting. Emily believes that the golf course pond behind our place has an alligator in it. That's why Louise and Emily go down and watch it with Emily's grandmother, Mrs. Timberstien, who is trying to teach Louise not to say "douche bag" or "jerk" or "butthole" so much. She doesn't like any of that language. And I agree they're bad, and I wish I hadn't used them in front of Louise, but I did and blame it on Missouri. Except Mrs. Timberstien survived the Holocaust, which is probably even worse than the Lake of the Ozarks, and somehow she never started cussing. She survived and came out like she's dignified.

Mrs. Timberstien makes Louise and Emily lunch and serves it on china with a cloth napkin and two forks, so that it looks like a restaurant. Plus she lights a candle. Then, in the afternoon, they usually go to the beach. I like that. I'm happy for Louise, because it's like Mrs. Timberstien is becoming her grandmother.

When we just arrived here, Fulton decided he liked the idea of a surfing career. He even bought a bashed-up fifteen-dollar surfboard at a yard sale. Unluckily, within a week he found out that the Gulf of Mexico doesn't have any waves other than the brand that hit your ankles. They're mini. So he's waiting for a storm. A few weeks ago, he came and asked, "Since I sometimes saved you from Dad, if a big storm comes, you wanna pay me back by going surfing?"

"I guess," I told him. I was watching television, the old *Bonanza* show about cowboys. There's a big father and his three loyal adult sons, one who is overweight.

I turned toward Fulton and indicated the television. "Hey, have you noticed? Hoss is fat but everyone likes him."

"So?"

"So, no one liked me when I was that way."

"That was just a few people. You only thought it was everyone."

I looked back at the television, and Hoss was putting a huge cowboy hat overtop the huge head he owned. Once it was set, it looked good. It looked perfectly normal on his block head and he was even handsome with his soft stomach.

I rested awake that night on the floor, my curtains getting moved by palmetto bugs, which are really cockroaches the size of a baby shoe. I despise palmetto bugs because they hardly die if you hit them with an adult shoe or a rolled magazine. Worse, they fly at you like birds attacking.

At first light, bright lizards appeared on my window screen, all of them wearing designs on their backs and stomachs. Some were green like the radiator fluid that comes out of our car or yellow or black and shiny like a polished car.

Two weeks ago, I was watching the lizards when the phone started ringing. In the kitchen, I said, "Hello."

"Cay! Son! I've balled all night, boy." It was my dad. He was being cowboy.

"Why?"

"'Cause'in Kora called me a drunkert and shut herself up in the boudoir. She says to me I'm losing my looks and my charm. Says I'm turning into a drunkert and a tax bandit with three redneck kids."

I didn't know what to say.

"Pardner?"

"Yeah?"

"Is it so?"

"You—you aren't a tax cheat, I think, and . . ."

He cut me off. "Do ya think I'm losing my looks and charm?"

What a question. Of course he was. I wasn't even sure why he was asking. He had strange, bumpy skin and no neck anymore. Also, his charm changed with his personality adjustments so that one charming personality never stayed long enough before it was replaced by one that was less charming and more mean. "No. Your looks and charms are fine."

"Ya sure, son?"

"Yeah."

"Well, goody. Hey, now, ya watching your weight, ain't ya? Ya ain't getting fat?"

"I'm not."

He said, "Stay, boy," like I was a dog and hung up.

I went back to my room and sat looking out the window again. I'd just talked to my dad, and I felt alright. My father's weirdness and comments hadn't pried open my heart and formed an expanding hole of lava and emptiness. My father was just my father. Nothing more. It was a good position for him to take.

A few days later, Fulton came into my room holding a bar of surfboard wax. "Guess what, Cay?"

"What?" I was drawing a picture of Spiderman slugging someone off the page.

"There's a storm, a tropical storm that might turn into a hurricane."

"So?"

"If there's a storm, we're surfing. You said you would."

I glanced back at Spiderman.

"It's for how I saved you from Dad sometimes."

"Oh, yeah," I told him, wishing I hadn't made the deal.

Two days later, Fulton woke me from my place on the floor. Outside, I could hear gusts of wind rustle all the bushes and trees between our house and the Timberstiens'.

I peered up at him. "What?"

"Waves," he said. "Surfing."

"But. . ." I pushed myself up. "Why so early?"

"So we don't get beaten for the good spots."

I breathed in. "We only have one board. Did you think of that?"

"We'll take turns."

"We don't have any life preservers."

"Surfers don't wear life preservers. I've been reading about it."

I got off the floor and wished for once that my mom or Henrico would wake up and walk into the kitchen. As loud as I could, I put on my swim trunks and one of my two short-sleeved shirts so that nobody on the beach would see any fatness on my stomach.

Together, me and Fulton fetched his big surfboard from the garage and headed down and around the dusky corner along Harbour Drive. The wind blew hard and rain came in little bursts. In the streetlights, it looked as if it was snowing. Anymore, I hated the idea of snow.

Crossing over the bridge, we went down to where the road intersected with Gulf Shore Boulevard. From there, we passed down a street that ended at the beach. All around, palm trees were bent over like boomerangs, their big fronds fluttering and cracking like plastic pennants. We walked beyond the wall that lined Naples's beaches, and onto the sand. Loose particles blasted painfully against us, forcing us to turn our heads and protect our eyes like we were in a camel caravan stuck in a desert sandstorm.

Fifty or so yards away was a lineup of tall, strong condominiums for old people who wore support socks and polyester shorts. I've seen them in the grocery stores. They buy a lot of stool softener and on-sale cookies.

Suddenly, daylight spread across the heavy gray sky from behind us, illuminating foamy cloud forms, all of them racing past. It also revealed the Gulf. The waves were monstrous. Ten footers roared in, whitecapping at a sandbar a few hundred yards off shore then rising again 'til they hit the beach with a "Whomp!" sound.

"Finally! Waves!" Fulton yelled.

I said, "No one else is here."

"That's 'cause we're first." He stripped off his shirt and shoveled sand on it so that it wouldn't tumbleweed down the beach.

I said, "Not even boats are out," and took off my shirt and buried it in the sand, too.

Struggling against the wind, Fulton carried his surfboard to the edge of the warm, foamy water.

I followed and went in so that I could hide my ex-overweightness if one of the old people was looking from their window. The stirred-up, green soupiness was like a bathtub, which made it feel safer than if it had been cold. Cold water, like in The Lodge by the Lake's pool, always seemed more scary to me.

Fulton said, "Let's hang ten!" He rushed forward and belly flopped onto his long surfboard, which went up and up a large wave before going down the backside. He put a rubber cord around his ankle that was designed to pull the surfboard back if he was thrown off it.

I dove in and passed under a big wave. On the backside, I stood on the bottom and felt the rip tide try and lift my feet.

Fulton paddled over a few more waves only getting flipped once. He righted himself and shouted back at me as I swam over them. "Let's get out to the sandbar!"

I nodded but wished I said, "No!"

Off he went, through the water, swells rising and falling in a disorganized way, bigger waves roaring in and bursting into foam that lifted in small pieces and flew down the beach.

Behind Fulton, my weak arms felt rubber-bandy almost right away, but I swam and swam and finally arrived at the sandbar, which we could just barely stand on between the waves that towered over us like greenish cliff walls.

"I'm going to surf one," Fulton called over the roar of water. He looked around carefully before he shimmied up on his long surfboard and paddled up and over the white wash of a giant wave. He waited carefully for a nice easy one to start up, then he took off, riding the board on his stomach. I didn't see him wipe out, but I spotted him as he struggled back.

It took a while for him to arrive, and when he did, he looked tired. Pushing the board over, he yelled, "I almost had a perfect ride, man!"

I put the leash on my ankle.

Fulton bobbed in place and steadied a hand to his brow, searching across the water.

"What?" I called.

He waited before saying, "Nothing."

I struggled up on the board and was suddenly carried halfway to shore before I was flipped and spun like I was caught on a paddlewheel.

Catching my breath, I started back with my arms trembling so bad it embarrassed me even though no one could see. Ahead, Fulton was disappearing and reappearing due to the breakers. Painfully, I struggled on, gasping and swallowing buckets of disgusting Gulf water.

"You didn't try to get up!" Fulton yelled at me when I arrived. Rain started showering down.

"I didn't want to." I gave Fulton the leash, my arms like lead.

He made a face and hesitated before strapping the leash around his ankle.

"What?" I called at him, annoyed.

He pulled himself halfway up on his surfboard. "It's nothing."

"What's nothing?"

"I just read that sharks sometimes get blown into shore during big storms!"

I nodded and spit, except no spit came out because I think I was suddenly nervous.

"I read it in *Surfer*. That's all. They write it in California, I think."

Concerned, I searched the waves around us.

Fulton called, "You wanna quit?"

"Maybe," I told him, wanting to say "yes" but not wanting to wimp out. I treaded up a wave. "If there're sharks, they don't scare me, but I don't wanna stay out here. That's all."

"Yeah…" he began, his voice trailing off.

"Stop it," I said, jerking around to look where he was looking and, like I was in a *Jaws*-the-movie nightmare, there was a huge shark silhouetted in a wave not fifteen feet away. The wave passed it by, and the massive man-eating carnivore disappeared below the surface of the water.

Terrified, I spun about hollering, "Fulton!" But Fulton was gone, probably chewed and swallowed already. Panicked, I started swimming and shouting for my brother. A wave glided up beneath me and I could imagine teeth sinking into my calves. From the crest of it, I spotted Fulton climbing from the water. He'd ridden the surfboard in, leaving me to get eaten.

Spastic, I went under and pushed off the sandy bottom. I thought about how unfair life was. I'd survived so much but was going to get my legs bitten off by a shark.

I pounded on, my arms instantly full of energy.

Not so far from shore, I caught a wave that carried me forward 'til my feet hit the sandy bottom and I was standing in water up to my knees. I ran out. Blowing sand hit me so hard it stung. Partway up the beach, I dropped to the ground, turned onto my back, and watched the sky that was leaking with yellow morning light.

Fulton arrived over to me. Squatting, he said, "Sorry."

I peered at him, but I wasn't mad. Instead, I smiled. I smiled a real smile. I don't know why, considering I'd nearly gotten eaten alive. But I did.

"Can you believe we saw that?" he asked.

"Not really." I rose onto my elbows. The sand hurt where it hit my body. "I got to get my shirt," I told him, suddenly embarrassed that he might see a wrinkle in my stomach.

"Blew away."

I glanced around. I didn't want to walk home with my stomach showing.

"I'm kidding. Here," Fulton told me, and held it out.

I put it on and stood. Fulton got his board, and, together, we started through the painful sand to the road. He spoke about stuff, but I didn't. For me, an enormous shark swam in my mind in and out of questions I had about who I had been and who I would become. The shark was less scary.

As Normal As We Can
Epilogue

When did my brain begin to unhook like the basement walls of our Missouri house? Thinking back past the darkness and the moving trucks, beyond Mrs. Morto's weak blatter and my first *Star Wars* figures, I remember not sleeping well before we moved to Norfolk.

In Yorktown, in the house we moved to after my dad left, I would be wide awake at two in the morning and pick up the phone to hear the taped lady operator say, "If you'd like to make a call." I never did but was glad for her question. Was I becoming unhooked then? In our two houses in Norfolk, I stole candy in my underwear from 7-11 stores and drank beer like it was Tab. How about then? I think maybe I was, partially.

Last week, me, Fulton, and Louise were walking through the Coastland Mall when Fulton said, "Mom helped me get a job at a pancake house."

"When?" I asked, stopping.

"While you and Louise were playing like two girls at Mrs. Timberstien's house the other day."

"I was being friendly," I explained.

"Whatever, huh."

Louise said, "So why do you want a job, Fulton?"

"For money and . . . to get away from you two. It's not normal for us to be around all the time. Don't you guys ever wanna be normal again? Don't you?"

I stopped and wondered how I could rise back to normalness after being so unnormal. I said, "Fulton, I—I thought you wanted to be a professional surfer, not a pancake server."

He bulged his eyes at me. "God, Cay, life is a long time. I've got years to serve tables and years to surf."

Louise told him, "I love pancakes."

I said, "I used to before my diet."

Fulton scoffed at me. "Cay, man. You know what? I'm so sick of you and your problems. I am."

I nodded because I guessed I was a little sick of them, and Fulton, too, making me think that I was actually getting more normal than I knew.

Suddenly, I stopped like I'd been secretly stapled to the floor. It occurred to me that our sorry trip, starting with my burping problem in Yorktown, to roughly that moment in the Coastland Mall, seemed to be coming to an end even if some of the effects lingered. For instance, I still get annoying insomnia, making me nervous that I could slide back to my unhinged ways of before. But I haven't yet. I guess when it comes to memories and brains everything heals slowly. But I could see, or start to see, that nothing lasts forever except maybe a winter in Missouri.

I said to Fulton, who was ahead of me, "I'm sick of you, too, you know. You're kind of an asshole."

He stopped and turned. Grinning cruelly, he said, "That's it, Cay. Keep talking, man. Get it all out of your system." And even though we were inside, he slid on a pair of red, devilish sunglasses like he was an animal who required darkness.

Louise wrinkled her nose at me. "You shouldn't use words like that."

Because I didn't want to upset her, I said, "Louise, I did it because we're acting like ordinary brothers and people again. We're finally getting as normal as we can."